FAIRY SUITED

Oak Fast Fated Mates Book 3

REBEL CARTER

For those who need freedom.

PROLOGUE

*O*nce there was a pack of greedy wolves who abused their mates and scoured the land looking for those they might steal and take for their own. These greedy wolves forgot their way beneath the moon and turned their backs on those that created them--the fey folk.

And for a time, they were successful. But greed is not a trait tolerated at large by the world of magic. That is an entirely Fey privilege.

And so, the Fey Queen stripped the greedy wolves of their magic, making them utterly ordinary.

But in this newly unmade pack, there was a female wolf, one that had no hate in her heart and was forced by those more powerful than she to do as they ordered. She, too, wished to escape them and their terrible greed. With all her heart she wished to be free, along with those that had been captured. It was in the aftermath of the Fey Queen's justice that she freed them. Then found herself at the mercy of a Fey Guard.

He should have punished her for her pack's deeds, but this Fey guard did no such thing. Could not, when faced with his mate. So, he spirited her away to a place only they knew, a place where she could live, grow and learn in safety.

But for all her new human nature, there was too much wolf left in the woman, and she longed to be free, had to be free in her new world.

Even if that freedom cost her everything.

Except, that everything to a fairy is nothing, if they do not have their mate.

CHAPTER ONE

Ximena glared at the sidewalk. She toed a crack in the pavement and added a frown to the mix. It wasn't that the sidewalk had wronged her, but it was the way leading her back to home. She shook her head.

No. That wasn't home.

She didn't have a home.

Ximena's hands balled into fists at her sides for a moment before she moved, thrusting them into the pockets of her hoodie. A raindrop landed on the sidewalk, another following in its wake, and then another, the smattering darkening the pavement under her feet. The rain was coming faster now, she could feel it through the thin material of her jacket, and she sighed, forcing herself back into motion. She had to get back...to her not home.

The hideout?

Safe House?

She shook her head at those. It sounded all wrong, like lines from the stuff she watched on the television. What she had waiting for her was more like a prison. She would be in trouble when she got back after *he* did. She walked faster now, knowing it was futile to think she would arrive first.

He being her self-appointed Fey bodyguard.

She should be grateful. She had thought he might kill her, but instead, he had hidden her away and kept her safe from her once pack mates. They had all but gone mad from losing their shifting ability. They'd royally fucked up when they had made the move to attack the Moon Claw pack, but her Alpha had been a cruel and greedy wolf bent on getting more mates for their pack. She wrapped her arms around herself, remembering her time with them. She hadn't always been a Bloodstone.

She'd been happy once, and free.

Until *they'd* taken her on one of their raids.

Ximena's head dipped, her chin hitting her chest as if shielding her from the memories of it. She'd been twelve, maybe thirteen, and shopping with her parents while on vacation. They must have scented her while she'd been trying to decide between a heart shaped purse or a turquoise sparkly set of sunglasses. She'd been so fixated on the items that she hadn't noticed them until it was too late. By the time she'd been able to scream they were dragging her out the back of the shop and shoving her into a waiting car.

She'd never seen or heard from her parents again.

Ximena hoped they were all right. It wasn't easy to be without parents, but she knew losing a child could break a family. She didn't want that to be the result of the Bloodstone's greed. They didn't deserve to have that power over her family, even if they had owned her for years. It had been a blessing to not find a mate in the pack. If she had, then her hopes of escape might have died a long time ago. And with it, her spirit.

Each day she remained unattached her will to escape grew until it was the only thing she had left. But then, things had changed when the Fey Queen had taken their magic.

Now her entire pack, all three hundred of them, were human and roaming the area, had been for weeks. That was probably a very bad thing for the residents of the quaint town the forest surrounded. She wondered how it was that no one had ever thought them capable of it.

Maybe it was because they had been without a Luna for so long, had no connection to the Fey. Not like the Moon Claw pack did. She supposed they should have known it was a possibility. Their actions were pushing them closer to punishment, especially with the way fairies could be.

Well, except for one fairy. *Her fairy.*

"He's not yours," she whispered, hands tightening so hard her nails bit into her palms. She had no business thinking of Blue like that.

He was most assuredly *not* hers.

He was her guardian.

5

But she was already working on a way to end that role. This couldn't go on forever. Ximena would be free, and Blue would be free to go back to whatever the hell fairies did when they weren't babysitting new humans.

She swallowed and quickened her pace, turning onto the street that would appear to dead-end, courtesy of Blue's fairy magic. Where normal people saw a dead end with a rotting tree, she knew different. He'd given her a charm to see past this particular illusion, and there, where the tree was for others, was the small house with its cheery yellow door, white shutters and blue clapboard. It would have been a cute little home for a happy couple, with its neat yard and small porch. But cute vanishes quickly when a house turns out to be less a home, and more a prison.

A prison just for *her.*

Though, the alternative was far worse. She wouldn't have survived out there in the woods with her pack mates. They had been cruel, but secure, as wolves.

As humans?

They would have been animals.

She winced and continued forward, legs eating up the pavement between her and the dead tree, then on towards the mocking yellow door. She knew she should be grateful to Blue, but it was...difficult, when they were isolated like they were. A shudder went through her in time with the shimmering air of her prison's boundary.

Ximena rolled her shoulders and shook out her

fingers, shaking off the excess magic that always clung to her from Blue's protection wards. She was still making a face at the lingering magic when the front door opened, and to Ximena's relief, she was able to keep a semblance of a poker face in place.

"Where have you been?" Blue arched an eyebrow at her, and Ximena looked away from those shimmering lavender eyes and down at her feet. Where she was stamping her shoes on the pavement a shimmer of gold fell to the ground.

"Nowhere." She added in a little bounce, the soles of her dark boots hitting the wet pavement with a satisfying thud.

"If you had been 'nowhere,'" Blue made air quotes with his fingers, and she couldn't help but roll her eyes at the human gesture, "then why are you coated in my magic?"

"Because fairy magic is like glitter," she bit out, still bouncing in place, "and it gets everywhere."

Blue huffed and took a heavy step out of the house and onto the porch, his black wings unfurling behind him with a stretch. Ximena kept her eyes down and firmly off the fairy's kick-ass wings, because truthfully...she loved his wings. Strong, and covered in sleek raven feathers that made her think of a moonless night sky. The kind of night she had loved as a wolf because it made her feel normal. The moon was not kind to weaker wolves, the urge to shift nearly uncontrollable. Full moons had been torture trying to keep her skin.

She would look at Blue's wings for way too many

awkward, uninterrupted minutes, if she thought she could do it without the fairy noticing. But he noticed everything, and she refused to even glance their way when he had them on display.

His flexed wings tucked in close behind him. She knew even without looking at him because Ximena too noticed everything.

Especially when it came to Blue.

The fairy was always a beautiful sight for her. Even if he hadn't been her mate, Ximena knew she would be captivated by him. He was tall, nearly a foot taller than her, in possession of chin-length white hair that sparkled like a moonbeam. It was pretty and lush, though the fairy opted to wear it tied back more often than not. He was muscular and broad-shouldered, though with an elegance she was certain came from him being a fairy and all. He could move as silently as a cat, one moment gone and the next beside her without her even noticing, which was insane to her. She, and any human, should notice when a blue-skinned fairy was on the move.

Especially one as large as Blue.

His skin reminded her of the blue hues of sunrise, the way the sky looked just before the first rays of the sun were noticeable. All of this and then some, with his angular jawline and high cheekbones, an aquiline profile and wide mouth she might have considered kissing more than once in the middle of an argument.

Blue was absolutely gorgeous. Even if it was diffi-cult to look at him when he was full on Fey, the way he was currently. When he was like this, it was like looking at the sun, and Ximena narrowed her eyes against the strength of all of Blue's full on fairy.

"Don't like my magic on you?" he asked. She grit her teeth against the fire she felt in her belly at his question.

"No," she lied, finally looking up to meet his eyes. Those were easier to look at. "You know it's hard to look at when you're all," she wiggled her fingers at him, "full-on fairy." It was hard to look at him even when he was human.

It was just fucking hard to look at her mate at all. Ximena was very aware that her situation was bullshit.

"Liar," he shot back, lips turning up in a smirk. "I can put up the human glamour for you, if you want," he offered, and she immediately shook her head.

"No, don't." Was all she said, and Ximena bit her bottom lip and held back the snide comment she longed to lob back at him.

If it was like looking at the sun when Blue was all fairy, it was nothing short of a full moon when he was in his human form. If Ximena had been a shifter still, she would have lost her skin at being found in front of a human Blue. That version of him undid her faster than she cared to admit, and excursions into town with human Blue were heart stopping. She'd rather it be like this, looking at him out of the corner of her eyes, or meeting his eyes in furtive glances.

Or glaring at him in frustration.

She didn't think their knack for getting under the

other's skin, while he was rocking his full human look, was going to do a damn thing for her keeping some semblance of cool.

Not when he was telling the truth. Because she was, in fact, a big liar. But that was what happened when fated mates were involved. And hers was currently standing in front of her in the form of a smirking fairy guard.

Blue skin, wings and all.

CHAPTER TWO

"I just don't like the way magic feels on me. It's like, like I can still shift even if it's only for a few minutes." Ximena looked away from Blue's dreamy, purple-hued eyes and concentrated on getting the last of the fairy magic off her and onto the ground, where it glimmered briefly like fool's gold. It would fade in a few minutes, leaving behind nothing to show it had ever been there.

She blinked, watching the gold shimmer in the dim light of the now fully-fledged rainstorm. Her clothing and hoodie were going to be soaked through in a matter of minutes, but she couldn't tear her eyes away from the glimmering magic at her feet.

When it was on her clothes, her skin, she felt like she was close to shifting. Like the ability was right there on the other side of an increasingly thinning veil. As if she only pushed hard enough she would manage to get through it and take what had once been hers.

Ximena hadn't always hated being a wolf, there were the times it had been sweet and hers, nothing but freedom. Even in those years when she had been claimed by the Bloodstone pack, Ximena had still managed to find a certain kind of freedom in her wolf form. Running until her limbs burned from it, the way the moon looked as a wolf, all sharp and pure light, the taste of a fresh spring on a hot summer night, or the way the wind sang to her when she was alone.

She missed those moments the most.

Human senses were too dull to find that kind of release, but that just meant she was going to have to be more direct in her bid for freedom. There would be no finding sweetness in captivity. This time she was going to have to actually get free.

That meant leaving Blue behind. Her stomach turned at that.

She looked at him, craving the sight of her mate at just the thought of running from him. When she looked his way she saw that Blue was still standing motionless on the porch, purple eyes glimmering for a split second as he considered her, before he moved forward and off the porch towards her.

"Come inside," he said when she made no move towards the house.

"I'm good." Ximena turned her face upwards towards the sky and smiled when raindrops hit her cheeks and forehead. There was a flash of light. Ximena didn't miss how the telltale gold glitter of Blue's magic joined the rain falling all around her. She bit the inside of her cheek knowing what he had done, and she shook her head.

"That's a dirty trick," she told him, opting to close her eyes when she heard him leave the porch to come stand beside her. He was tall, but not now as tall as he was when he was fairy, standing just a few inches taller than her. His hair was shoulder length, dark brown, thick and curly. She would give anything to twist a lock of it around her fingers.

He was muscular, but the kind of muscle that made her think of speed and grace, rather than brute strength. Tan skin, high cheekbones, a lush mouth any woman would have a hard time not falling in lust with, and the hint of stubble along a strong jaw completed the picture of her mate.

Except...*except,* then there were his eyes.

Those purple eyes she was most familiar with, sharp and seemingly all seeing. He never missed a beat, and it kept her on her toes.

She adored his eyes.

You know, when they weren't trained on her like they were now. She swallowed and glanced at him before she turned her face back to the storm.

"A very dirty trick."

"It's not a trick, just my human form." His tone was teasing and light, at odds with the hunger for him that had a nasty way of reawakening any time she caught a glimpse of Blue's human side. He knew how much it affected her. Sometimes she wondered if he wanted to go on supply runs simply to drive her crazy with want.

"You're annoying," she told him.

"And you're headstrong," he replied. "What a pair. Now come inside before you get sick."

"I'm not going to get sick. Wolves don-" her voice broke off in the middle of her sentence, the words dying on her lips as soon as she almost uttered them. Words that were no longer true.

"Wolves might not get sick, but humans do," Blue replied, knowing what she had nearly said. He put a hand on her wrist and tugged her forward. "Come inside with me. Don't fight it."

Her breath caught the second his fingers brushed her skin and she jerked as if touched by a live wire.

"That's not fair," she breathed, but came forward all the same, trailing behind Blue.

"I don't play fair, you know that, Xi."

She rolled her eyes at his use of the nickname he had taken to using over their past weeks in hiding. She'd never had a nickname before, not as a child and not with the Bloodstones. She was happy, happier than she should be, that Blue had given her one.

"Whatever," she grumbled, following Blue onto the porch and into the house. The door clicked shut behind them and Ximena shivered against the chill that had begun to settle into her bones. Blue had been right, any longer outside and she would have gotten sick. Life sucked without her enhanced immune system. Wolves didn't get sick, ever, but she wasn't a wolf anymore. That had been one of the reasons, other than her safety and fated mate status, that Blue had brought her here.

She'd needed a safe space to learn how to be human. Blue was insistent on her mastering the fine art of mundane human life, no magic in her life whatsoever. *Why* Blue was so focused on her being able to pass as human, she wasn't entirely sure...though if she thought too long on it, she was faced with the truth.

He aimed to leave her, eventually.

Sacrificing a mate to gain the freedom she craved wasn't exactly how she had imagined her life playing out, but here she was.

Blue wouldn't stay, and she wouldn't go back to being a shifter.

And that's just how it was.

That didn't mean she wasn't doing her damndest to prolong the whole thing. She knew well enough that Blue wouldn't leave her, not until he was sure she had it all down. You know, whatever *it* was.

The whole human jam.

She nearly wrinkled her nose at the thought. She wasn't human. Didn't want to be, but if it were the road to freedom then what else could she do?

Nothing.

Nothing but eke out a little more time with her mate. She hadn't really done so well on her end at mastering the fine art of everyday human existence. Ximena did her best not to think too hard on the why of that, or what her days would be like without Blue to simultaneously annoy and lust after.

"We need to get you warmed up, Xi." His hands rubbing against her arms jerked her back to the present and she blinked up at him, her cheeks heating as he continued to touch her. "Give me your hoodie."

"I'm fine," she said, wrapping her arms, and her jacket, tighter around her body.

"It's soaking wet. You can't keep it on."

"But I--"

"Off, Xi." He made an impatient gesture with his hand and she rolled her eyes at him, even as she began to strip the hoodie off.

She huffed. "You're so bossy." She handed him the soaking hoodie and stepped past him towards the living room, but an 'ahem' cough from him stopped her in her tracks. "What?" Ximena raised her eyebrow, looking over her shoulder at him.

He pointed down at her shoes. "Shoes. Socks."

"You know what, I don't think it's normal for human men to be this bossy," she informed him, taking off her shoes.

"Good thing I'm not a human," he told her wryly, watching her get her shoes and socks off.

"No, but I am," she reminded him. "And if you want me to be able to function in the real world as a human, then I should probably be around a more human-natured, well human. I need to be around real human men, Blue. Don't you think?"

He scoffed and came forward suddenly, surprising her so much that she backed up into the wall with a thump. But Blue's focus wasn't on her. It was on her soaking shoes and socks. He bent low, snagging the boots and socks from the wood floor and added them to the hoodie over his arm.

"There's no reason for you to become accustomed to human men."

Her brow wrinkled and she pushed herself awkwardly away from the wall she had just crashed into. "What's that supposed to mean? All you want me to do is adjust to human life. You've made that very clear since you found me, and guess what, Blue? Men account for about half the population out there. Just because I got kidnapped when I was a kid by a bunch of psychos doesn't mean I forgot that much. How am I supposed to understand male attention and behavior if you're always telling me what to do?"

He raised his eyes and she shivered when his familiar eyes hit hers. Even in his human form, Blue's eyes were the same, that beautiful lavender shade that stopped her in her tracks any time the pair locked eyes.

"Human world or not you have a mate. Human men do not concern you, Xi. The only male attention you need to understand *is mine.*"

A familiar flutter in her belly stirred to life at his words and she had to fight against crossing the hallway and flinging herself at him. She could not do that. She'd done it once before, and in that rare and tender moment when her control had been non-existent, he had set her straight on what he was—on what they were meant to be. She couldn't allow that to happen again, not when she already knew what would happen if she reached for him.

So instead she looked away from him, her eyes sliding away to a spot just to the side of his head. She was silent for a long beat before she finally swallowed and spoke.

"You make no sense, so I think I'd rather focus on learning what human men are about."

He smiled at her, the slow and sad kind, before he sighed. "I'm going to get these dry. There's tea in the kitchen, and I've got a fire going in the living room if you want to read in there." He left then, striding down the hall and to the left where the small laundry room was.

Tea, a crackling fire, and reading while a storm raged outside? It was a perfect afternoon to Ximena, one that she had always dreamed of while being stuck with the Bloodstones. It had been nothing but work, obedience, and obligations where they were concerned. They never had cared about the quality of her life, or any of the other taken female wolves. It had at least been tolerable as an unmated wolf. The lives of the mated She-wolves had been even worse. Raising pups and being chained to an unrelenting mate was no way for a free wolf to live. For years Ximena had lived in fear of finding her mate, each time she was dragged in front of a new alpha had been a cause for fear.

But then...but then, she'd found *her mate.*

And he hadn't been what she'd fear. No, instead, he'd turned out to be beautiful. And kind, caring, and attentive. Even if he was pretty damn bossy.

She smiled and watched Blue's back for a second before he entered the laundry room and vanished out of sight. What he was doing in there when she was sure he could just magic the clothes dry was beyond her. Her mate was nothing to be scared of, even if he wasn't hers to keep. A heavy sigh escaped her lips, but she pushed down the melancholy the thought of losing Blue brought to mind, and made for the promised tea in the kitchen.

She poured a cup and inhaled the scent of chamomile with a happy sigh. She could hear Blue working in the laundry room, the sound of him adding a happy hum to the notes of the rain pouring outside. She closed her eyes briefly, leaning into the cozy domestic feel of the home.

Home...

"No, it's not a home." She opened her eyes and shook her head, her cup hitting the counter with a clang. What the hell was she doing? "This is a slippery slope, Xi. Cut it out." She mentally shook a finger at herself and snatched up her cup of tea. She chose to ignore the fact she had referred to Blue's nickname for herself.

She wasn't supposed to do that. Just like she wasn't supposed to think of this place as home.

It was a prison. A halfway point. Simply a resting place on her way to wherever her human life took her. Blue would be back to his fairy life then, and she wouldn't have to guard herself around his human form. Her heart pinged painfully, and she gripped her cup tighter.

She was going to hate life without Blue.

She was frowning and angrily snapping open the book she had been reading the previous day when Blue entered the living room. He paused in the doorway and considered her for a second before he asked, "What's wrong?"

"Nothing." She turned the page with a tad too much force and the fairy pursed his lips.

"What's with all the lying today, Xi?"

"What's with all the questions today, Blue?"

"Wouldn't be asking so many if you were being honest."

Ximena hummed but said nothing, her eyes on the pages in front of her. It was a romance novel. She'd been fond of them before she'd been taken, or at least she had remembered being so during her time with the Bloodstones. She'd snuck more than a handful of them away from her mother's collection and had devoured them way past her bedtime under her heaviest quilt to hide the light of her flashlight. She'd daydreamed of those nights while with the Bloodstones, longed for them. It had been a no brainer when Blue had asked her what kind of books she wanted him to bring her.

It had only taken a couple of paperbacks and her expectant looks for him to begin bringing her into town with him so that she could grab every last book that caught her attention. She hadn't strayed from romance books, not yet.

After all this time she needed the assured happy ending. It didn't matter what the state of the story was at the beginning of the book, she knew that by the end of it everything was going to work out-there would be a happily ever after.

It made her feel safe. She craved that sense of security. To know there was nothing to worry about, even if there were challenges and bumps in the road. Romance books, for the time being, scratched her itch for happily ever after.

Ximena shifted, yanked a blanket over her legs, and settled back onto the sofa with a contented sigh. She had just begun reading when Blue entered the room, a cup of tea in hand. His eyes landed on hers the second he hit the threshold.

"Is the tea good?" he asked, taking a seat across from her in the armchair beside the fireplace.

"It's, ah, yummy." She looked at him over the top of her book and saw that he was still in his human form. "Why are you still human?"

He shrugged and lifted his cup of tea to his lips and took a sip. "I think I might stay like this for a while."

She frowned. "Why?"

"You look upset."

"I'm not," she lied.

"You're lying a lot today. Why is that?"

"No, I'm not." She shut her book with a snap and ignored that she was, *again, lying.* "But why aren't you answering my question? What's the deal?"

"Deal?" Blue gave her a look that could be none other than feigned innocence. "What are you talking about, Xi?"

"The human getup. You know that it--" she stopped

abruptly, and then swallowed hard. She couldn't finish the sentence she had just been about to blurt out, even if he knew what it was. What she had nearly said.

Blue's eyes shimmered and he smirked at her. "What were you about to say?"

"Nothing." She yanked the blanket tighter over her legs and willed herself to think of anything other than how much she wanted to climb into Blue's lap.

His smirk turned into a grin and he looked away from her and to his cup of tea. "You said you wanted to get used to human men, remember?" he reminded her. "I figured you getting used to seeing a man would help you with acclimating."

She sat up straighter and gave him a wide-eyed look. "That isn't what I meant, and you know that. Anyhow, you said I didn't need to know what human male attention was like. Remember that?" she shot back.

He chuckled and raised his teacup to her. "Right, I did. And I was also right about that. You don't."

"Then how exactly is staying in your human form helpful?" she asked, hating that it was affecting her so much and so quickly too.

"It will help. Trust me. I quite like this form. I had just been staying away from it for...certain purposes."

Her mouth pursed and she shook her head, looking back at her book's pages. "Right, and by 'purposes,' you mean that I want to crawl all over you, don't you?"

He tipped his head towards hers in agreement. "Correct."

Her mouth fell open. She hadn't expected him to agree with her. She had thought he might deny it, claim that she was being dramatic or that it was all silly. They hadn't, until that moment, said aloud what the effect of Blue's human form had on her.

Goddess knew that Ximena didn't exactly have anyone to discuss her innermost thoughts with, seeing as her social circle consisted of Blue, and *oh, yeah, Blue.*

Ximena had thought to take it with her to the grave. She had prayed Blue hadn't caught on. Until just now she had figured the fairy had remained blissfully unaware, but she should have known better. Blue noticed everything, cataloged and organized carefully until he needed to use the information.

It appeared now was Blue's determined occasion to drop such knowledge, and she glared at him.

"Whatever," she managed to splutter. "Change back."

Blue laughed, the kind of laugh that filled a room and warmed a girl as thoroughly as any roaring fireplace or hot cup of tea. Ximena wished she didn't notice that, but she did. Blue's lavender eyes moved slowly over her until they met hers.

"I'm staying human."

"But I-"

"I'm staying human, and it will be for the best. It will help everything." Blue leaned forward, elbows braced on his knees, watching her as he spoke, "And that's it, Xi. Understood?" His voice had lost all of its normal lightness. There was no teasing now, or warmth. No, that gentle touch Blue had to him had deepened until the warmth was a raging flame, setting her on fire from head to toe.

There was no room for arguing. Not now. As much as Ximena hated it, she could see that Blue was going to win this round.

For the best or not, he was going to stay human. And, at least for now, she wasn't going to have one thing to say about it.

CHAPTER THREE

The afternoon had passed companionably enough. They had drunk their tea with Blue rising every so often to stoke the fire or add to the logs while Ximena read. Thankfully, Blue hadn't pressed the issue on where she had gone, and dinner had passed easily as well with Blue making her favorite —macaroni and cheese.

It had been one of the last things she'd enjoyed with her family, and the first meal she had requested when she realized Blue actually cared about what she wanted. There had been little conversation, a rarity, but Ximena didn't question it.

Instead she had been glad for fewer opportunities to spill the beans on where she had been. She didn't really feel like explaining the why of her journey into town to see for herself if the place she had heard the Moon Claw Luna was working at was real, or not. A magic coffee shop? She'd never been in such a place as an adult, where witches, shifters and humans all existed and worked together. She didn't know why, but she knew she had to get to the shop. Had to get the Luna on her side.

There was a pull there. If she did, then somehow, her life would be closer to getting back on track. She didn't know if it was a human, or shifter life, but it was worth a shot. Ximena had spent much of her life fighting what she was and resenting it. But now...now she had a chance to let it guide her. And it was demanding she make it to the coffee shop, so that's exactly what she was going to do.

She just didn't want to tell Blue about it. Not yet.

Ximena was quite pleased with how dinner and the day had gone and was just about to slip upstairs when Blue cleared his throat and stopped her.

"Where were you?" he asked, effectively squashing her high hopes of escape.

"Nowhere," she insisted.

He tossed the dish towel in his hands over his shoulder and crossed his arms, the muscle in his forearms flexing in an awfully distracting way. She licked her lips and forced her eyes to Blue's and not on his temping arms.

"Try again, Xi."

"On a walk, Blue. I was on a walk because it's-it's hard to be here all the time, alone."

"You aren't alone. You have me."

She shook her head and glanced towards the stairs. "You know what I mean, Blue. I'm supposed to be getting acclimated to being a human, but how am I supposed to do that if I never see any?"

He was silent then, lips pursed, and she didn't miss the way his jaw clenched slightly. Blue blew out a sigh and took a step closer to her, a movement she mimicked in reverse, her shoulder glancing off the doorway as she moved. She stumbled, an arm going out to steady herself as she moved into the hallway.

"Fair point," he said. "And that is why I'm staying like this." He flicked a finger at himself.

"Like what?"

"Human."

She frowned at that and then sighed. "You know what that does. I'm giving up trying to understand fairies, you're impossible...or is it just *you* that I don't get?"

He paused considering her question, and then sucked on his bottom lip, the slight gesture something that plucked at Ximena as surely as she imagined a harp string might when played upon—true and undeniable. His eyes hit hers and she saw they were darker hued than their normal light purple. They were a deep indigo, nearly black so deep had they turned, and she shivered at the sight of it.

This was need and longing, she could feel it rolling off of him in big waves that would drown her if she just gave in. She couldn't go under the tide of his need, not when she knew he would leave her, that whatever this was between them would not be hers to keep.

She'd only seen Blue look at her like this once before.

The night they had met.

Ximena had wanted Blue from the first. Had known he was her mate in those fleeting moments when she'd literally ended up at his feet. The battle around them had raged on that night. The battle had been wrong, but no one had listened to her.

Instead she'd been forced to come along with them. When Ximena had seen an opportunity for escape, she had run. But just as she had bolted one of her pack mates, a bully Alpha she had always loathed, had spotted her and given chase. As if trying to escape hadn't been enough, she'd now have to attempt it with a pissed off Alpha on her heels. An Omega was no match for an Alpha, they both knew it. She was pretty fucked, but Ximena had always been one to cling to hope, and so she had run on through the forest with the Alpha crashing through the trees behind her.

She'd run as fast as she could, her lungs and legs burning from it until she'd tripped, like an idiot, over a tree root of all things, and gone tumbling down face first into the dirt. Ximena had known, even lying face down, that she wasn't alone. That there was something else there, something other than the Alpha, about to grab her.

"Mate." The word had been uttered in a growl that resonated through her bones, as if pulled from the earth beneath her, and Ximena had gasped. A hand beneath her chin had tilted her face up and she could see that it wasn't just any something ready to pounce. It was her mate that was now here with her. That moment had seemed to go on, the Alpha behind her suddenly falling back with a yelp from whatever magic her mate had almost carelessly aimed at him with a flick of his hand. What happened to her once pack mate was a mystery, but Ximena hadn't cared, still didn't, in fact, because Blue had been there.

"Help me," she whispered, covering his hand at her chin with her own. "Don't let them hurt me."

Those indigo eyes-those eyes that burned with a need she knew as surely as her own breath, because it was now moving through her unchecked-had gone light suddenly at her plea. The fairy in front of her sucked in a shuddering breath, and with a shake of his head he moved his hand to take hers.

"We're leaving."

They'd vanished then. The next thing Ximena knew, she was standing with Blue in front of the home she now shared with him. When she reached for him he had shied away from her with a rueful smile and urged her forward.

"It's best we get you indoors before your where-abouts become known. It will be safer later, but now…" he paused, his voice trailing off as he glanced towards the house, "now, we need to be smart. Follow me. You're safe now."

And that had been that. The lusty feelings Ximena had to beat back, those dark urges that made her want to climb him, kiss him, oh hell, just touch him, were seemingly hers alone to struggle with. Even as they argued and bantered with each other day-in-and-out, her fairy caretaker had never shown romantic interest in her. Blue had been polite and helpful, protective when she worried, and always a steady presence. But this look, this use of human form in an almost aggravating way, was definitely new.

He liked to tease her, nothing more. But those dark eyes said something else entirely about Blue's motives in staying human. And that mouth? Moon goddess help her, she needed to get away from him before she did something completely ridiculous.

Something she couldn't take back.

She swallowed against the feeling and took a hurrying step, first one and then another, towards the stairs until she was halfway up the staircase when Blue finally answered her.

"It's just me, Xi. It's just me."

❦

Ximena hadn't gotten any sleep. Okay, that was a stretch, she might have dozed off somewhere in the night, but it had only lasted until she'd ended up dreaming about Blue. The fairy had been human and smoking hot in her dreams. He had been downright seducing her with a kiss that she'd woken from feeling achingly frustrated. She rubbed at her mouth and sighed. It was aching to be kissed, just like the rest of her was crying out for...for...something.

"Blue, you want Blue. Just say it," she groaned, grabbing the pillow to the side of her and yanking it over her head. Her mind, body, and most recently, her mouth, wanted the fairy. With a sigh, she sat up and swung her legs over the bed. She needed to get up and fake her way through a normalish day if she was going to shake her fairy thirst.

"There's nothing wrong with wanting your mate," she reminded herself as she brushed her teeth and washed her face. "It's normal. Perfectly fucking normal," she said, exiting the bathroom and walking smack into Blue.

"What are you doing out here!" she screeched, jumping back and banging into the bathroom door.

Blue was standing in the hallway with a towel thrown over his shoulder and a hand in his hair. He rubbed at it and gave her a raised eyebrow. "I was waiting for the bathroom, but you were in there talking to yourself."

"I was not talking to myself."

"What's perfectly normal to want?" he asked.

Her eyes widened. Of course the damn fairy had heard her trying to give herself a pep talk.

Damn it. Damn it. Damn it.

"Pizza for breakfast. Jalapeno and pepperoni."

"That's really what you want?" She nodded. Blue pursed his lips and then sighed, shaking his head at her.

"Humans are strange. I'm not sure that's perfectly normal."

"Says the fairy parading around as a human," she pointed out nodding at him, and he shrugged.

"You like me better this way," he replied and stepped around her into the bathroom. "Breakfast is ready, so why don't you stop monopolizing the bathroom."

Ximena opened her mouth to say something back but then snapped it shut. He hadn't pushed her on her response, so why try her luck?

"Fine, fine." She threw up her hands and moved out of the way and down the hall towards the stairs. She stopped and looked back at him before going too far, to see that he was watching her from the bathroom doorway. "Thanks for breakfast, Blue." His smile was warm as the sunshine in spring and she softened at the sight of it.

"Any time, Xi." He pointed a finger down the hall and jerked his chin towards the stairs. "Now hurry up, I want to head into town, and you take forever eating."

"It's called *savoring* my food."

"Whatever." The door slammed behind Blue and Ximena rolled her eyes and turned back to the stairs. She wondered what Blue would be after this early in the day in town, or why he would want to leave so quickly.

She stopped short when she entered the kitchen to see that on the small breakfast table they shared there was a box of pizza at the center, with a plate and silverware next to it. She looked up at the ceiling when she heard the shower go on and huffed out a laugh. She opened the pizza box to see a freshly made jalapeño and pepperoni pizza inside.

"Fairy guards. Always keeping a girl on her toes," she murmured, pulling a slice of the pizza Blue had apparently magicked out of thin air for her breakfast. Sometimes he got on her last nerve and then other times, he did this. It was sweet. She bit into the pizza and moaned. She was still exploring food options now that she wasn't with her pack and pizza was always a delight, especially this pizza.

Her absolute favorite.

She had managed to eat half of the pizza by the time Blue entered the room freshly showered and toweling off his hair. Ximena's eyes lingered on the dark curls for longer than they should have as she ate her final piece of pizza.

"Breakfast good?" he asked, filling a cup of coffee and watching her as she ate.

She nodded. "Thank you for the pizza. You didn't have to do that."

"You mentioned it. You know I always want to give you what you want." He sipped from his coffee mug once more and then made for the door. "Let's get a move on. I have a couple of stops in town, I'll take you to the bookstore first and circle back for you."

"Wait, where are you going?" she asked. "Why aren't you eating anything for breakfast?"

"I ate earlier, Xi. Get your shoes on. Grab your jacket. It's been raining."

"Stop being so bossy!" she called out to him from where she still sat at the table.

She heard Blue chuckle by the front door, and then he said, "No."

Ximena smiled in spite of herself and rose from the table to put away the pizza before she hurried after Blue. He was already waiting for her outside on the porch, the door was open, and the fairy cut a fine sight leaning against the porch railing, sipping his coffee in the early morning light. Ximena worked to keep her balance while getting her fill of fairy eye candy, which really just amounted to her hopping awkwardly on one foot, then the next as she yanked on her boots. She snagged her jacket on her way out and joined him on the porch. Blue was staring out across the neighborhood, his eyes focused on something she couldn't see.

She stepped close and looked where he was gazing but frowned when she didn't see anything out of the ordinary. Just the same houses, cars, and the normal early morning going ons of a neighborhood. A gray cat hopped off of a car hood and meandered down the sidewalk on a morning jaunt.

"Where are we going?" she asked, watching the cat.

"*We* aren't going anywhere," Blue told her, blowing on his coffee. "I'm going on errands, and *you*," he said, stressing the word you in a way that aggravated Ximena to no end, "are going to the bookstore."

"But I want to go with you," she blurted out. She snapped her mouth shut with a gasp as soon as the words left her mouth and cleared her throat. "What I

mean is that I want to, ah, I don't know if I want to..."
her voice trailed off and she crossed her arms over her
chest, eyes still on the cat that was now making its way
towards the dead tree that marked their boundary. It
stopped and daintily sniffed at the tree before it turned
and walked away, Blue's magic no doubt repelling the
cat. It had an off-putting effect on animals and humans
alike, making them steer clear of the space even though
there was nothing to their eyes beyond the tree.

"Don't want to what?" Blue asked. He was looking
at her over the rim of his coffee cup, and she didn't
miss the way his eyes narrowed.

"I don't know," she admitted and shook her head
with a sigh. "It's nothing," she continued after a beat
and gave him a tight smile. "Let's go," Ximena said
quickly when he moved to stop her. She hopped off the
porch and made for the direction of town before he
could stop her, and before long she heard his footballs
behind her, and then beside her, as they walked into
town.

"I won't be long, but if my errands take longer than
I expect you should go on and get some lunch without
me."

She stuffed her hands into her hoodie and looked
up at him in surprise. They never ate without one
another. Rather, they were never apart long enough to
eat without the other. Since Blue had found her they
had been nearly inseparable. Though that had mostly
been on account of keeping her away from her former
pack mates. She bit her lip and looked beyond the

houses on their left. The forest was close to them, it was close to everyone and everything in Alaska. This neighborhood was the same as any, and here the trees and underbrush butted right up to the yards and houses. They turned the corner and she reached out, catching a handful of fir needles as they passed, and she smiled at their rough touch beneath her fingers.

"You never miss lunch," she said, pulling a fistful of fir needles off the tree.

"And I shouldn't today either, Xi. It's just in case."

"Oh, all right. Even if you won't tell me where you're going." Ximena dropped the fir needles to the ground, wiping her hands against her jeans.

"It's not that exciting, I promise," he said, continuing down the sidewalk. "Let's get moving. I know how you get when you're in a bookstore."

She hummed in answer and went to follow after him but a movement in the trees made her freeze. Ximena squinted and stared. Her human eyesight wasn't quite up to where her shifter sight had been, but she knew she had seen something in the trees. And whatever it was...didn't move right. Not for the forest animals she was familiar with.

"What the hell?" she whispered when she saw it again, but this time it was farther away. A shadow slipping along a tree, so slight a movement that she would have missed it if she hadn't been looking for it. She took a step into the trees, watching as it dropped down into the underbrush, the leaves rustling as it cleared the space and began to move.

Ximena pushed into the trees, eyes locked onto the shadow? The figure? What the hell was it? She could feel her curiosity roused, that part of her that didn't quite understand she wasn't a wolf anymore springing to life and demanding that she give chase, if for only the sake of satisfying her curiosity. She had just begun to drop into a low crouch when Blue called out to her.

"Where are you going, Xi?"

"Shhh!" she hissed, freezing because the dark shape also froze. She could hardly see it now from where she was.

"Get back here!"

"Stop ruining my fun," she shot back and then groaned when the shadow bolted. Tree limbs and bushes shaking as it ran deeper and deeper into the forest. Blue's hand closed around her arm and pulled her back when she considered giving chase.

"Where are you-what are you doing in the forest?" he asked, pulling her around to face him. "You know it isn't safe for you in here."

"I'm fine, Blue. It was just that that something was there."

"Where?" Blue looked past her, eyes scanning the trees for what she had seen, and she pointed.

"There, there was something that way but I couldn't see where it went because," she pointed a finger at her eyes in annoyance, "my eyes are bad."

"Your eyes aren't bad. They're perfect."

"Stop that."

"Stop what?" Blue wanted to know. Her heart sped

up at those two simple words, because he was definitely doing *that thing* he did with his voice that made her lose focus on everything and anything that wasn't related to Blue. *That thing* being when he spoke in a low voice, the one that made her think of thunder rumbling behind dark clouds before a storm overtook her. The voice that hit her straight in the chest and filled her until she felt like she might stop breathing from the ache of it. All she wanted to do was wrap herself around him and just *be*.

But she couldn't be.

Not when Blue was going to leave her. If she let herself get close, if she gave into *that thing*, Ximena was only making their inevitable parting harder than it needed to be. And that was why she couldn't do this, why she needed to get away from Blue.

She took a step away from him then, her feet moving before she could think better of it. Blue frowned at her movement, but she pretended not to notice, narrowing her eyes in a feigned search for the shadow that had seemingly melted away into the forest underbrush. She blew out a puff of breath, pushing her hair off her forehead with a shake of her head.

"There was something there," she told Blue.

He tilted his head to the side, eyes drifting closed and was silent for a moment. "I can't sense anything, Xi. There are lots of animals in the forest. I'm sure it was just one of those." Blue's hand was on her arm then, and she nearly jumped at the light touch. "Xi, it's okay, are you all right?"

Ximena bit her lip and shied away from Blue's touch when he made to step closer. Distance was good. She could do with some distance from Blue.

"I'm fine," she told him with a tight smile. "Let's get to town...you had errands, right?" She did an about face from the forest and tramped through the trees until her feet were back on the pavement. She rocked back on her heels and waited until Blue joined her.

The walk into town was short, which was thankful because it was also quiet. Normally, silence between them was nonexistent, and when it happened it was peaceful, but this? This quiet was heavy, restless even, and she knew Blue wanted to say something.

But what? She couldn't imagine, but that was mostly for the fact that Ximena had no way to put into words what was bothering her, or why she had been so intent on figuring out exactly what had been in the forest. She felt unsettled. She glanced nervously his way and blew out the breath she hadn't known she'd been holding in when the bookstore came into sight. She relaxed the moment she made it to the front door and paused there when Blue didn't come closer.

He always came with her, at least to start. She shot him a curious look. "What is it?"

Blue gave a quick shake of his head. "It's nothing. Go on in. I'll be back before too long but remember if I take longer than-"

"Then expected then go on and do lunch without you," she finished for him, and he gave her an approving smile.

"Exactly, Xi. Make sure you eat if I don't see you. Go ahead and hang out in town, I'll find you when I'm ready to head back."

She raised an eyebrow. "Really?" she asked, in surprise. Since she'd become human, she had hardly spent time on her own at their home, let alone in town. All of her excursions had been done seemingly without Blue knowing-though she was becoming sure the fairy knew about her trips.

Blue inclined his head. "Really. You deserve some alone time at your favorite place in the whole world."

She grinned and took a step back gesturing at the bookstore. "That's because this place has it all, Blue! Baked goods, books, and a comfy couch. There's even a shop cat in here! Who wouldn't love this place?"

"A fool," he replied. Blue loved the bookstore as much as she did, and the pair of them had spent many an afternoon picking out books. It was then that she liked Blue's magical fairy touch. You didn't have to worry about a book budget when you were with a fairy. Whatever the total, Blue always had the exact amount they needed. She would definitely miss that when they parted ways. He nodded at the bookstore. "Go on in, I'll be back for you in a while. But if you get hungry go ahead without me." He repeated.

She paused and gave him a considering look. They had always stuck together, but here he was leaving her to her own devices in the bookstore, and now lunch?

"Is it safe?" she asked, hating the tremor she heard in her own voice.

He nodded at her. "Yes. We haven't heard from your pack in weeks. We won't be like this forever."

Her heart thumped awkwardly in her chest. If they weren't like this forever, then they would be apart. Ximena didn't like to think of that, so instead, she put a fake smile on her face.

"Sure, see ya." Her voice was chipper and upbeat, a mask for the way she truly felt. She would focus on the positives. Blue was here with her now, the sun was shining, and she had a morning ahead of her in a bookstore.

It was a good day. She would hold on to that. And so she waved at him and before he could look too deeply, like the fairy was prone to do, she darted into the bookstore and made straight for her favorite section in the shop.

The Romance section.

It didn't matter what kind of romance it was, Ximena loved them all. She loved the bad boys and the cinnamon rolls, the enemies to lovers and the grumpy ones that loved the sunshine ones.

All of it.

Romance also helped Ximena fill in the gaps of her knowledge on how the world worked. Or at least gave her the expectation for how the world ought to work. Walker Books was a treasure trove of reads and she never was disappointed in the selection of happily-ever-afters available on the shelves for her.

She crossed her arms over her chest and considered the books in front of her. The brightly colored spines and pretty fonts were always a treat to look at. What would she read today? She had just reached out and plucked a book off the shelf, a sports romance from the amount of well-honed abs and hockey sticks across the cover, when a girl popped her head around the corner.

"Hi there!" She waved at Ximena, causing her to jump at the other woman's sudden appearance.

"Hi, ah, hello?" Ximena tried, clutching the book to her chest.

"How are you? Can I help you with anything?" Her eyes went to the book in Ximena's hands and she hummed in approval. "That one is real hot," she said pointing at the book excitedly.

"Is it?" Ximena looked down. "I've never read anything by this author."

"Oh, well you are in for a treat, because," the woman looked around the store before stepping around the bookshelf and towards her, lowering her voice conspiratorially, "this woman knows how to write some dick."

Ximena burst out laughing. "Then I'll take it. Thanks for the hot tip."

"Any time, I'm here to help guide each and every romance lover to the right happy ending. I am honor-bound to ensure this section's success. Do you even know how much I had to argue with my dad to expand it from a few crappy copies of some pretty problematic shit?"

"Your dad?"

"Oh!" The woman put a hand to her chest and then

gave a little bow over it, "Allow me to introduce myself. My name is Toni, short for Antonia, but no one calls me that but my dad when he's ticked. We own the shop and I work here. I've seen you around before, but you're usually with…" her voice trailed off and she looked over Ximena's shoulder, scanning the rows behind her, "you know, that hottie with a body. Your boyfriend."

Ximena nodded, knowing very well what Toni meant. "That's Blue. He's got some business to do today, so I'm solo for this trip."

"Hmm, no eye candy then," She sighed and leaned against the shelf.

She gave Toni an apologetic smile. "'Fraid not." She stopped then and held up a hand, processing what Toni had just said. "Wait, my boyfriend? No, he's *not* my boyfriend."

Toni raised an eyebrow. "Has anyone told *him* that?" she asked.

"What do you mean told *him*?" Ximena wanted to know. Suddenly the sports romance in her hand wasn't as compelling as it had been a minute ago. "Spill," she ordered.

"Ooo, you're direct. I like that. I like that a lot." Toni grinned at her and then continued when Ximena gestured impatiently at her. "All I'm saying is that the boy was looking at you like you were good enough to eat, and if he's not your boyfriend then I don't think anyone gave him the memo."

"What are you—I mean, I don't know what you're

talking about," Ximena spluttered and turned to grab another book from the shelf. This one had a medieval maiden on the cover, and what looked to be a sword-wielding warrior bent on wooing her. She bit her lip and considered it, she had never really read a medieval romance but there was a first time for everything, she supposed. "Say what do you think about this one?" she tried, but Toni waved her off.

"Don't try and change the topic, woman! Let's stick to where I'm enlightening you about your not-boyfriend's feelings for you! Feelings that are very, very boyfriendly."

Ximena blushed hot and looked back down at the book in her hand. There was a kilt involved, so she decided she didn't need a recommendation to decide to buy it. She was taking it. She tucked it under her arm and cleared her throat, "Okay, well I'm Xi--"

"Getting off topic."

"No, I'm Ximena. I was going to at least introduce myself if you're going to tell me about my love life."

Toni winced and slapped her forehead. "My bad. I totally just steamrolled you. I have a way of doing that sometimes when I get excited."

"And Blue and I excite you?" she asked.

"Uh, duh, this is Alaska in the middle of nowhere and my dad doesn't let me talk to the fairies in town. Of course you are exciting!"

She bit back a smile at Toni's long-suffering expression. If only she knew that Blue was one such off limit fairy.

"Thanks," she paused, and picked up another book from the shelf beside them at random. Hmm, vampire romance. She made a face, putting it back, "I mean, I think?"

"Vampires not for you, eh?"

Ximena shook her head. "They're not the nicest."

Toni's eyes widened with interest. "What?"

"Ah, nothing, nothing. I mean, they aren't written the nicest," she lied. Ximena's opinion on vampires was entirely born of first-hand experience from her time as a shifter. They were high-handed and kind of snotty. At least they had been to her, but she couldn't tell Toni that. Not if she intended to stay in Oak Fast. She paused at that and considered it. Would she stay in Oak Fast after Blue left her? Or would she move on? And if she did move on, where the hell did she plan on going?

"Something tells me you aren't being entirely truthful, but that's okay, Ximena. We just became friends so the good dirt takes time. I can respect that."

Ximena opened her mouth to deny that she was holding back on the hot vampire gossip, but Toni shrugged it off. "Talk to me about this man. Blue, you called him?"

"That's his name, yeah. And he's my friend. Just a friend."

"That old song and dance, hmm?" Toni hummed and nodded sagely. "Classic. I get it, but he's into you, and I thought you were into him too? Or was I reading that sparkly magic wrong?"

Her eyebrows shot up into her hairline and Ximena

nearly dropped the books in arms. "What do you mean sparkly magic?"

Toni was silent for a second before she cleared her throat and pushed away from the bookshelf to stand up taller. "You know the name of this book store is Walkers Books, right?" Ximena nodded and waited for Toni to continue on which she did after licking her lips and casting a furtive look behind her and around the bookstore. There were only a few patrons in the shop and once she saw they were not listening she beckoned Ximena closer. "That's because my dad and I are Walkers. It's not really our last name. I mean, it is, but isn't... if you know what I mean."

"Yes? No.I mean, no I don't know," Ximena admitted.

"It's more of a job title than a surname is what I'm trying to get at here. We are Walkers. As in, we get to do the dimension skip and hop dance all we want."

"The what?"

"We get to go between dimensions."

"Holy shit."

"Yeah, it's a trip." Toni wiggled her eyebrows and leaned closer with a smirk. "Like literally, it's a trip. The whole thing is one big trip. You wouldn't believe the places I've ended up on accident. The shit I've seen." She shook her head and blew out a sigh that told Ximena that Toni had indeed seen some shit.

"I've never heard of Walkers before."

"That's because there aren't a ton of us, and it's one of those need-to-know basis sort of things."

"But you told me," Ximena pointed out.

"That's because we're friends," Toni reminded her.

"But we just met."

"Yeah, but I like you and I have a good feeling about you. We're going to be awesome friends, I can tell! Matching tattoos, the whole thing."

Ximena blinked at matching tattoos, but she couldn't deny Toni's energy and enthusiasm was...infectious. It had been a while since she'd had time with other women, time that wasn't spent doing some crappy task or chore under the watchful eye of her pack mates. Blue was good to talk to, he was fun to hang out with too, but it wasn't the same as being around another woman.

She had missed this sort of thing. She figured, why not trust Toni's feeling about her? How else would she go about making friends? It couldn't possibly get any easier than this, with Toni offering her friendship up on a silver platter.

"Okay, we're friends."

Toni looked at her in surprise. "Really? Just like that?"

"Yeah, why not? Just like that." Ximena stopped and considered the question. "Is it usually harder to make human friends?"

Toni clapped her hands. "Aha! I knew it! You aren't human! But like," she scrunched up her nose, "you are?"

Ximena laughed nervously. "Why would you think I'm not human? I am so *totally* human."

"Because humans don't say 'human friends', they're just friends."

Ximena sucked in a breath ready to tell Toni just how wrong she was but she stopped, because...*well...yeah.* She had a point.

"Well, you got me there," she admitted.

"So what are you then? You seem more human than not. I was thinking maybe Selkie, but then you ripped on the vampires and I thought okay, maybe not?"

"Do Selkies like vampires?"

"Those two are a match made in heaven. Didn't you know?"

She shook her head. "Can't say that I ever knew that, but there's a lot I don't know."

"Because you're not human."

She laughed and pressed the books closer to her chest. "I am human, Toni. That's the thing."

"Why is it a thing? Human is sort of the default setting around here, but you aren't on that wavelength..."

"That's because I wasn't always human. I was," she swallowed hard and the words got caught in her throat before she could say them. This was the first time she had discussed her once shifter situation with anyone that wasn't Blue. It wasn't like she had friends. Toni was her only friend, and it was a relationship of all of five minutes. Before this there had only been Blue, which she knew wasn't great but what could a new human on the run and trying to learn the ropes do? "I was a wolf once."

Toni's eyes went round, her smile vanishing in an instant. "You were a shifter? And a wolf?"

"Yeah, but some major shit went down and my pack lost their powers for a serious fuck up. I got lumped in with them, and here I am. I'm just trying to learn how it all works out here."

"Out here being the human world?"

She nodded. "Yeah, the guy you've seen me with, he isn't my boyfriend. He's more like a guard."

"A guard? What are you, some kind of princess?"

Ximena bit back a laugh. "No, I'm not a princess. But Blue is a guard. Or was? I'm not sure, he hasn't been clear on it since we got to Oak Fast. He found me and brought me here. My pack, ah, my old pack is out in the woods causing trouble. I wasn't exactly welcome there or valued either. They took me when I was a kid, so I wasn't true pack. Which meant I'd be catching the brunt of whatever they were mad about. Blue thought it would be better for me to learn how to human without them around."

Toni nodded slowly. "That makes sense. I'm sorry your pack was shitty. No, they weren't just shitty, they were moon touched."

"Thank you. I'm glad that's over now." An onslaught of memories, or rather feelings, hit her full force at thinking about her old pack. Those had been hard times, full of misery and longing to be free. She was nearly there, and things were certainly better, but it didn't mean thinking of them or what had been didn't sting. She blinked rapidly against the tears burning the back of her eyelids and dropped her gaze to her shoes.

"Hey, come with me," Toni murmured, reaching forward to touch her elbow. Together the women walked until they were around the corner and in a small reading nook Ximena had used on more than one occasion when she had wanted to be alone with her recent purchases.

"You okay?" Toni asked once they were sitting facing each other knee-to-knee.

"Yeah," Ximena blew out a shaking laugh. "It's fine, I'm getting better. It's just that sometimes it all comes back and hits me, and it sucks for a little while, you know?"

Toni rubbed her shoulder gently and hummed sympathetically. "I'm sorry. You shouldn't have gone through that. Are they the ones skulking around the woods?" Toni asked, her warm brown eyes dark with concern.

"Yeah, that's them." Ximena replied automatically but as the words sunk in she sat up straight and the books she had still been holding fell to the floor."Wait, what do you mean? You've heard about them?"

"Yeah, everyone has. I don't know what they're doing. I mean, most people here think they're just a weird gang of squatters, but I know that isn't right. It makes sense they used to be wolves from what I've seen." She reached down and snagged the books up from the floor and placed them back in Ximena's lap.

"I'm a Walker, remember? I walk. It's what I do, and I see things. I know those people aren't *people.*"

Those people aren't people.

Ximena's blood ran cold, and she bit her lip. "They're dangerous."

"Figured."

"I have to tell Blue." She made to stand and Toni reached out a hand to stop her.

"Make sure you check in with me here, okay? You've got a friend that's going to worry about you from now on."

Ximena could scarcely stop the smile on her face. A friend. She had one. She *was* one. "Of course. I'll make sure to stop back in this week."

"Perfect. And take the books. They're on the house," she said, giving Ximena a gentle nudge towards the door. She held up a hand when Ximena made to protest. "Look, you've got a lot going on, and when I say a lot, I mean a lot. You have a shitty pack of feral humans roaming around that you have to stay clear of, and then there's the whole not boyfriend guard situation? Take it from your new best friend, you need that stack of books. Take them."

Ximena chuckled as they walked on through the store. The other shoppers were blissfully unaware that a Walker and a once wolf were in their midst, let alone had just become best friends over a stack of romance novels. To them it was just another day of shopping, but to Ximena it was the start of her very first true friendship.

Today was the best.

They paused at the front door and Ximena held the books up, giving Toni a thankful smile. "Okay, maybe you're right. I do have a lot going on. Thank you. I appreciate this, new best friend."

Toni beamed at her. "Thank you for enabling me. Too many people don't and it gets boring." She opened the door for Ximena and nodded out at the street. "Go have fun with your not boyfriend, and if that doesn't work out remember, at least we have book boyfriends!"

Ximena gave her a salute and hopped out onto the street. "Thanks for the advice. I'll keep that in mind. But we are *just friends*," she said, stressing the words, to which Toni snorted.

"Sure, cupcake." Then the door was closing and Toni gave her one last parting wave before she vanished back into the shop. Ximena stared at the closed door, there was a lightness in her chest that hadn't been there before.

Friends it seemed could work a magic all their own.

CHAPTER FOUR

W hen Blue got home, he did it the human way. It was a change from the fairy way he came and went usually, which consisted of him stepping out of the room and vanishing from plain sight, even while still talking to Ximena. He would blink back into being and surprise her at random when he returned, picking up the conversation right where they had left off. She hated that at first but it had begun to grow on her as her new normal, part of their routine over the last few weeks. That made seeing him arriving home in his human form all the more out of place.

Ximena looked up from the book she was reading, the medieval one--turned out she had a real big thing for men with broadswords and accents, but then again, who didn't? She glanced out the window and saw Blue ambling up the pavement in his human form. Ximena watched him walking with the normal grace she was used to seeing as Fey, but there he was, still human, a fact that stood out all the more with the unnaturally smooth way he moved. No one could see him and think he was only human. Why was he still at it? Why had he chosen to stay human for this long? He'd never done that before, not that she could remember. Fairies did nothing without cause. There was a reason, she knew enough about the Fey to know that much. So when he entered the living room she asked, "What's with the human get up?"

He shrugged. "I like it."

"You walked home," she pointed out.

"Sure did." Blue sank down onto the couch across from her and nodded at the book in her hands. "What's that? Looks spicy."

She blushed but held the book aloft, proudly displaying the bare-chested warrior to Blue's gaze. "It is and it's superbly written. A true literary gem of an adventure."

He chuckled and rested his chin in his hand. "You like men that look like that?" he asked.

"What?" She froze where she was, book above her head, feet in fuzzy socks and tucked under her. "What do you mean?"

"The man on that cover. Is that what you like?" Blue was curious.

"Why do you want to know?"

"Just making conversation." He gave her an innocent smile and she frowned at him, knowing that his smile was anything but, which meant his question was also not for the sole purpose of making conversation.

"You're lying."

He blew out a sigh, eyes rolling briefly before he leaned forward and looked at her. "Yeah, I am."

"Then what's with the question?"

"I was curious about what my mate likes," he replied, his voice dropping a touch from its normal smooth tones and it was then she heard the rasp in it. She had only heard that tone from him once before. The night they had met. He'd only said one word then.

Mate.

Goddess, she remembered the sound of that voice, the way it moved through her and over her until it had her feeling like she was coming apart and coming together all at once. Blue's voice had been the key to it, that roiling heat that took what it wanted and left her shuddering on her hands and knees on the forest floor.

And it was here again.

But now...now things were different. They had weeks of time between them, of time spent with the other, of time she had been sure he was about to leave her. Except, the voice was back. It was back, and he was calling her his mate while he looked at her like a starving fairy.

She leaned back in her seat at seeing his eyes darken, their normal lavender deepened to a nearly black blue.

"What is-" she began, and then faltered, "Why do you care?" she finished lamely.

"One should know what their mate prefers, but..." he bit his bottom lip and nodded at the book she was holding, "as good as he looks, I think you like me better."

When she said nothing, Blue moved, going to his knees in front of her and making her mouth fall open in shock at the sudden change in position. How had they gotten here? With him looking up at her like she was the answer to everything, while she was wearing her fuzzy socks and reading a highlander medieval romance?

"You do like me better, hmm?"

Toni was right. She did have a lot going on.

"I like you both fine," she replied, clearing her throat. "Do you want me to get a start on dinner?" She made to stand, but Blue extended his arm to the side of her, his hand splayed across the burgundy material of the couch, and she swallowed hard.

Blue had big hands. Big, beautiful hands.

"I don't want you to like us both fine," he said.

"You don't?" She watched as his hand moved towards her until it stopped, hovering over her side. He paused there and she held her breath.

"No," he said, and then added, "I want you to like me the best."

His hand was still there, only inches from her side. She knew if she leaned into it she would have his hand on her, but she remained where she was and so did Blue. The pair of them locked into a game of chicken neither seemed willing, or ready, to break.

"You do?" she asked, voice barely a whisper. Outside the rain was falling harder now and a clap of thunder made her jump slightly, the book falling to the side, her place forgotten in favor of staring into Blue's eyes.

Big hands. Beautiful eyes. This fairy had her right where he wanted her.

"I want to touch you, Xi."

Her breath caught. She hadn't expected that. She looked down to see that he hadn't moved a muscle, those fingers and that big hand she had just been admiring still almost touching her, but not quite close enough.

"May I touch you, Xi?" He was waiting, she realized. Her heart began to beat out a staccato rhythm that forced her chest to rise and fall faster. How was he having this effect on her? She felt the familiar pull of their bond working on her, forcing her to lose all sense when it came to Blue. Except...except that when it came to the fairy, she found she didn't need to be forced at all.

Not even a little bit.

"Yes, you—"

A crash so loud it shook the house interrupted her words and they both froze. The delicate web of energy, the feel of their bond solidifying between them twisted and snapped out of existence. She would have sworn if she wasn't currently trying to figure out if the house was going to fall on them.

"What the hell was that?" she exclaimed, hands

yanking the blanket closer as she shrank into the couch.

"My wards," Blue said, standing up from his place and making for the windows. "Something triggered them. Wait here." There was a shimmer and a ripple and suddenly Blue was in his fey form, all blue skin, black wings, and narrowed eyes.

"But Blue, what--"

"Don't go anywhere. I mean it." He pointed at her. "Stay put. I'll be back. Do not open the door for anyone. Do you understand?"

"Yes, Blue."

"Good." And then he was gone, the familiar vacuum that accompanied his blinking out of one place to the next hit her, and she clenched her hands on the throw blanket over her legs. She wished she was with him, that she wasn't a human, but a wolf capable of watching his back. As it was, she simply had to wait here for him to return, and hope for the best.

"This sucks," she muttered after a few minutes of silence. She scooted closer to the edge of the couch and sighed before she finally stood and made for the window. Blue had said not to move but staying in the same room was the same thing, surely. He couldn't have meant exactly where she'd been, could he?

When she got to the window she saw there was only blackness in front of her. The porch light was currently on and so was the light at the end of the corner of their road. Both lights did precious little against the falling night and onslaught of the storm's darkened skies. The other houses on the street were dark, their porch lights out, which was, in her estimation, odd. The residents of Oak Fast, both supernatural and not, had a habit of lighting the way home at night. All these dark homes were not normal. Not even a little it. Someone, or something, was pushing on the boundaries of Blue's magic.

Another bang rocked the house and she yelped, hitting the floor in surprise. No, it wasn't normal. Certainly not with Blue's wards going off like they were.

"Please stay safe," she whispered, pushing herself back against the wall. She would stay put like he told her. It was all she could do, wasn't it? She was tense, waiting for another sign Blue's wards were being tested. But instead of a warning she heard something else. The sound of feet. Feet on the stairs, moving fast and without any thought to stealth. The footsteps kept coming, rocketing across their porch until a hand slammed on the front door.

Someone was knocking, no, banging, for her to let them in.

A whimper fought to free itself from her throat but she fought against it. She had to stay calm, she had to stay strong, she was not going to be afraid. No, she was done with that. Done being afraid. Even if she were a human she would do her best. She growled, the sound weak in her throat, but the familiar rumble of it was enough to force her to her feet. She grabbed the fireplace poker from its place and turned towards the hallway. Blue had said not to open the door to anyone but....

BANG, BANG, BANG!

There was that.

The house quaked, another resounding *boom!* made her flinch and look towards the ceiling.

And that.

Something was seriously messed up and she couldn't sit here pretending it was all fine. She had to check out the front door. She adjusted her grip and stepped out into the hallway. "You can do this," she coached herself, walking towards the front door. It was when she got there that another thwack against the door made her jump.

She blew out a breath and paused, raising a hand to unlock the door. "Who's there?" she tried, instead of opening the door outright. Blue had to give her points for that if he got angry at her, right?

A moan on the other side of the door made her blood run cold. It was a moan she had never heard before, but it was certainly a voice she had. Seeing as she had only made her first friend that day, and this was a masculine moan, there could only be one being capable of that sound. One fairy to be specific.

"Blue!" she cried, unlocking and yanking the door open without a second thought. The fireplace poker hit the floor when she took in the sight of her mate slumped against the side of their home, blood coming from his chest and arm.

"Oh no, oh no," she whispered, reaching for him

before wincing. Her hands slid in his blood, but she didn't let go of him. Instead she adjusted her grip and pulled him back towards her. She had to get him inside before whatever had done this to him came back.

"Blue, can you hear me?" she tried, managing to drag him back a foot into the house. He slumped back, his shoulder smacking her in the face as she struggled to stay upright. "Blue, answer me!" She gave him a shake when he didn't answer right away, but when she dropped him clumsily on the floor in her attempt to close the door he groaned, eyelids fluttering open.

"You weren't supposed to open the door," he told her with a grimace.

She shoved the door closed with a slam of her shoulder. "And if I hadn't opened the door then what? You would still be there bleeding out on the porch." She ripped open the button-up flannel Blue wore, making him hiss in pain. "I'm sorry," Ximena whispered and then cleared her throat, trying to stay level headed. There was so much blood and she wasn't used to seeing him like this. Blue was always so strong and sure of himself, and now he was on the floor barely able to lift his head. There was so much blood.

"Xi, it's going to be okay," he raised a hand and put it on hers. "Just give me a minute and---"

"It's not going to be okay, you're hurt! Now tell me what to do!" Her heart was thumping wildly, she could feel it in her chest. A loud screech signaled another attack on the wards. Whatever was out there was still trying to get in, still pushing against Blue's magic and now he was hurt who knew how long it would hold? She sucked in a breath and stared at her mate. He was injured, she was practically useless outside of her skills with the fire poker she had dropped on the floor, and there was something trying to get inside the wards. With Blue's magic no one or no, well, anything, should know they were there.

Whatever was outside had been looking for them. For her.

Goddess, this was all her fault.

"Xi, look at me," Blue squeezed her hand. His touch was light, weaker than it normally was on the rare occasions they did touch, and her heart dropped. If it had been capable of leaving her body it would have landed between them, shortly followed by her stomach.

Blue shouldn't be weak, his fingers shaking as they tightened on hers. This shouldn't be happening. What if—what if she never got to know what it was like to be with him?

He was her mate. How could that be? She wouldn't let it, *couldn't* let it be the end of whatever it was they had, or didn't have in their case as mates. Even if it was for just a second, Ximena was going to know what it was like to give into what she wanted.

And what she wanted was Blue.

Blue sucked in a shallow breath and opened his eyes to look at her. They were beautiful. Lighter than normal, like the sky before sunrise. Would they see it? Or was this going to be their last night here? Their last night together?

"Xi? Are you—"

She shook her head and reached for him, bloodied fingers touching his hair gently and shocking him into silence. They stared at one another for a beat before Ximena mustered up her courage and did the damn thing.

She kissed Blue.

Time stopped for Ximena with that kiss. There was no softness to it, just eager, wanting, and needing. And Ximena took what she needed from the kiss. She took until she was left breathless. Her heart was beating louder than the sound of the wards, or the storm outside. None of it touched the wildness awakened in her from kissing Blue.

And Goddess, he was kissing her back. His hands were in her hair pulling, the strands twisting round his fingers as he slanted her mouth to his and took as equally as she did. The push and pull of them, a dance that morphed and tangled them up in one another until she wasn't sure if it was her chest that rose, or his.

"Blue..." She was breathing hard, eyes squeezed shut from what she had just done. Because she wouldn't take it back. Not in a million years, not ever. Didn't mean that she was eager to look him in the eyes quite yet. She was scared of what she would see in those lavender eyes, worried over what those would see in her.

"Blue, I—"

"You're mine," he rasped, fingers flexing against her scalp. Just those two words. Two words suddenly shifted her world in a way she hadn't thought possible, and the breath she'd been holding whooshed out of her in a sigh.

She opened her eyes.

"Yes."

He kissed her again and she felt the curve of his lips push up into a smile. "My mate." The words hung between them and she smiled, placing her hands on either side of his face. A spark flew from her fingertips to his skin, the small charge making her gasp.

"What the hell is that?" she asked him, jerking her hands back.

"I thought that would happen," Blue told her with a huff of laughter.

"Thought what would happen?"

"We're super charged, Xi."

"Sorry, we're what? Super charged? What does that even--"

A crash overhead interrupted her, and this time she nearly rolled her eyes at the sound instead of worrying. Whatever was out there was getting on her damned nerves now, not frightening her. She didn't care if she was human, she was going to make whatever was raising hell out there and messing up her first kiss with her mate, pay. The how of doing that escaped her, but it was coming quick, fast, and in a hurry.

"I'm going to beat them silly," she said, glaring at the ceiling.

"I wouldn't, ah, count on that. But the sentiment is nice, Xi," Blue grimaced when he moved, and he lowered a hand to his abdomen, the abdomen that she had just been trying to get to until she'd lost her head and kissed the fairy.

"Fuck. You're hurt." She shook her head at herself. "I forgot. I'm sorry," she reached for his shirt. "Here, let me take a look at it."

"Xi, it's fine."

She pulled a face. "What do you mean *fine*? Fine is-is...okay, I can't think of anything right now! Because there's something," she flung an arm out towards the door, "trying to get in here! And we just kissed, and that made a spark! A spark, Blue. And all of that together would be, I don't know, fine. But you're bleeding! All together, the sum of it does not equal *fine*, Blue."

She reached for him, the need to do something, *anything* ,so great that she just had to try and start somewhere. Blue caught her hands in his and pushed himself up with a slight wince. "I'm going to be fine, I'm already healing."

"But the blood--"

"Is from before. Can't get it off me or the shirt, but fairies heal up fast. I just need a few minutes." He rested their intertwined hands against his stomach, eyes closing, and Ximena frowned at the sight. She hated seeing him like this.

"What did this to you?" she opted for when she couldn't find anything else to say, or do, that Blue would allow. The fairy had a vice grip on her and didn't seem inclined to loosen his hold.

"No clue." He opened his eyes and looked towards the door. "Whatever it was, it was fast. I think," he paused and narrowed his eyes, "if it's what I think it was, or could be, it isn't good."

"Why?"

He moved to stand then, and when she tried to protest he waved her off and slapped his stomach with a resounding smack that made her jump. "I'm good as new. No need to fuss, Xi."

She scowled at him. "Stop hitting your stomach like that!"

"But it's fine, and if I don't show you I'm healed you'll worry." He caught her hand in his and raised it to his mouth, brushing a kiss against the knuckles. "I hate it when you worry."

"I don't worry," she told him.

Blue sighed and tucked a lock of hair behind her ear. "You do. All the time."

"How did you know that?"

Outside a clap of thunder sounded and then there was a flash of lightning, the burst of light worked to cast her mate's features in stark contrast to the soft glow of hall lights. He was so beautiful...and he was hers. He smiled at her, a tender one that she felt right down to her toes and he stepped in close. It was then she remembered she'd ripped open his shirt and felt her mouth go dry at the picture he cut. Even covered in blood, her mate was still smokin'.

Well hell.

"I can feel it," Blue replied, voice so soft she might

have missed it in the hum of the storm if she hadn't been listening for it. "It's constant. I wish...I wish you didn't worry so much."

"I worry about us," she blurted out.

He froze, shoulders tensing at her words. "What? Us?"

"I worry about what will happen when you leave me. What I'm going to do when I'm supposed to just be human without you."

"Why would you..." he took a step closer then and caught both of her hands in his, pulling her forward until she was against his chest. "Why would you ever think, in this dimension or the next, that I would leave you?"

"Because you kept saying when 'I was human,' and telling me I would have to adjust to life without your fairy hoodoo."

He rolled his eyes. "It's not 'hoodoo,' it's *arcane knowledge*. You know I hate it when you call it hoodoo."

"Whatever, it is. Your fairy ass tinker bell hoodoo. You said that I had to learn to be full human, and that was the whole purpose of this." she gestured towards the hallway, a motion that was hampered by the fact that Blue did not let go of her hand and they both ended up flailing to make her point. "Why else would you tell me that if you weren't going to peace out once I got the hang of it?"

Blue gave her a pained look. "Maybe because I never said, 'hey, Xi, learn to be human because I'm going to leave', now did I?"

"That's not the point."

"That is entirely the point." This time it was Blue that flailed a hand, taking hers with him in a wild swing. "I do not understand you, humans. Not even a little bit."

"Hey, I'm barely human."

"Fine, new humans. All humans. You're all leaping to conclusions like you're some red-capped toadstool."

She scrunched up her face. "Like a what?"

He flailed again, both arms this time, and Ximena went up on her tiptoes to keep up. "It's not important."

"Then what is?" she asked, tossing her head back to clear the hair from her eyes. She needed her eyes to be ready and focused, otherwise she might miss Blue's next wild gesture and then she'd be flat on her ass. She didn't think flat on one's ass was really a position conducive to a serious conversation.

"That I am not leaving you." He moved then, their arms once more following the same movement, but this one was to bring her close, pulling her hands around his back so she was hugging him. Ximena could have just stood there, her arms around her mate, cheek pressed to his chest. She could hear his heart thumping against her ear, could lose herself to that rhythmic beat that grounded her. But she didn't.

Instead, she leaned back and raised her face to look up at his. She wanted to look at him, she'd spent far too long unable to. Too long looking at him from the corners of her eyes or stopping herself from lingering on him. She had told herself it was because he was too beautiful, but it had never been that.

It was because she had never thought him to be truly hers.

But now? Now he was. He was utterly and perfectly hers. She squeezed him tight and smiled when he grinned at her.

"I am never leaving you," he told her again. She believed him.

CHAPTER FIVE

I t should have been sweet. Those initial minutes in admitting their bond to the other, the first of all touches, those early kisses, but it was hard for anything to be magic when wards were being set off like a summer meteor shower in full glory. She scowled and looked away from Blue when the wards blared again.

"You know what? I *wish* it would get in, with all this noise it's causing."

"You *would* say that."

She arched an eyebrow. "What's that supposed to mean?"

"Just that you're a wolf where it still counts." Blue grinned and leaned close, kissing her mouth. It was just a quick peck but it made her feel warm and happy, and the scowl vanished from her face. "Come on, I think I know what's going to send our friend out there a clear message."

She took his hand and fell into step beside him. They were heading towards the basement, but she was less focused on where they were going and more on what it felt like to hold Blue's hand. He had good hands. She knew this, had known it for quite some time but now, she was experiencing it. Damn was it nice. She squeezed his hand tighter in hers. She could get used to this. "Okay, but you never told me what did all of this to you," she jerked a chin at his bloodied shirt.

"Oh, this."

"Yes, 'oh this'. Now, you pretty much know everything—"

"I don't know everything."

"And I take you not knowing what the hell hurt you as a big what-the-fuck-oh-no moment."

Blue sucked on his bottom lip and stopped in front of the basement, his free hand resting on the door knob. He was silent for a second before he sighed and said. "It's not that I don't know what did it. I'm just not sure exactly. If it's what I think then we are in big trouble."

"That isn't clearing up the big-what-the-fuck-oh-no moment. I just want you to know that. In fact, you've managed to add an even bigger 'oh no' right on top of it."

"That doesn't help, does it?"

"Not at all."

"Shit."

He jerked open the basement door and nodded in

front of him as he switched on the light. "Go on down. We are going to see what we're dealing with."

Ximena hated to let go of his hand but she knew if she didn't it was going to make for an awkward trip down the basement stairs so she sighed, let his hand drop, and made her way down the rickety stairs. Blue followed her down and before long they were both standing on the packed dirt of the basement. She kicked at the floor and then gave him a 'what now?' look when he did nothing but stare at her.

"Uh, hello?" she waved a hand at him and he laughed.

"Sorry, it's just nice being able to look at you without worrying you'll run off," he said.

"I did not run off," she called after him when he stepped around her and made for the closet located at the back of the basement.

"Sure you didn't. Don't think I didn't see it, or how you wouldn't even look at me." He opened the closet and squatted down, eyes on the floor in front of him as he spoke. "You were very bad at trying to hide it from me, Xi."

The 'it' was her behavior. The way she'd distanced herself, kept him at arms length to protect herself from the hurt of losing him. She had felt that her mate had rejected her in all but name. She had embraced her need for freedom, made sure to hold fast to the urge to escape that had taken root and sprung up as eagerly as any tree in early spring. And like a sapling, her need for space and freedom, to escape her circumstances before she found herself at the mercy of a broken heart.

A heart broken by a mate was unfixable. All shifters knew this and it was not a lesson she forgot even though she was now human.

"We're leaving."

Those had been the only other words he'd said then, fingers skimming her chin as she lay at his feet asking for his help. He had helped her then, but they had gone no further. She had thought it was on account of him leaving her to her own devices, to adjust to her now human state and then be rid of her. But now? Him leaving had been the one imminent thought—the all important ending Ximena had felt sure of. But where she had imagined Blue and her leaving to find their own paths, it seemed that now leaving would be an adventure they would take together.

And as much as it made her glad, made her heart feel as if it might burst from the fullness of it she hated that it had taken a shitty night time attack and her mate bloodied and nearly unconscious for her to take the leap of faith being mates required. But Ximena had been low on faith, that special sort of magic mates existed in. Her supply of faith had been nearly decimated by her time held by the Bloodstones. They had worked to kill that part of her, and as much she hated to admit it, they had gotten far closer to succeeding than Ximena liked to admit.

Ximena had been running scared since they had taken her from her parents. What she hadn't realized was that she had never stopped. Not even in all the days since she had left with Blue, and maybe not even now, either.

But she would stop running. She had to. But how?

Her hands twisted together and she took a stutter step towards Blue where he was hunched, hands in the dirt, head bent towards his work. How would she stop running? How would she give in to hope well and truly? Then, it had been easy to keep going. Then, all she had had was the slight touch of his hand on her chin, that one single touch shared before he had spirited her away to their now home.

She couldn't accept the bond and let him close on the merit of a single touch.

Now they had a kiss. A confession. The promise of tomorrow. Ximena fought the urge to pull away, to run, even with the pull of their bond growing stronger by the second.

"I thought you were leaving," she said, voice dropping so suddenly it cracked. Blue's shoulders stiffened, hands going still in front of him. He had been drawing a series of sigils in the dirt there, but he turned away from his work with a furrowed brow.

"I— he began, but then stopped speaking and cleared his throat, "I could have handled it better."

"Why didn't you?" she asked, her voice still hardly above a whisper. Overhead the wards blared, the harsh sound of it deafening but even through the noise she made herself heard, "You never told me different. You knew I couldn't look at you, but you allowed it. Why did you—why wouldn't you tell me that you would not go?"

Blue stood. He wiped his hands on his jeans and moved to take a step towards her but stopped himself. "I did not want to trap you. I knew you wanted your freedom, and I felt the decision should be yours and yours alone. Fairies, all Fey folk, influence those they speak to. I could not risk it with my mate."

"What do you mean influence?" Ximena had learned little of fairies as a shifter. The Bloodstone Pack had never been in tune with the moon goddess and the knowledge of fairies had been reduced to a handful of myths pack members scared one another with before bed.

It was all of the usual gossip: fairies were monsters, beings that took what they pleased, fairies could not be trusted. Ximena had even been told that fairies were compelled to gamble, that they were unable to refuse a game when challenged.

So far Blue had turned down her efforts to swindle him at cards, and he had refused her invites to play any of the board games she had found in the house. She couldn't so much as entice the Fairy to take her on in a round of Hungry, Hungry, Hippo.

Who didn't like feeding brightly colored mammals courtesy of button smashing? It had been one of her favorite games as a child, and she had been ecstatic to find it in the house. Blue's uncultured taste in games had disproven the fey folks need to play games. So what did wolves know on the matter of fairies?

Apparently nothing, herself included.

Blue splayed out his hands between them and said, "Influence. As in fairies get what they want, even when we do not choose to make it so. If I want something and I speak with any being, supernatural or not, it would be near impossible for them not to be swayed. What I want would be what they want. Humans are most susceptible to our charms."

Ximena blinked. "Are you saying that you—you didn't clear this up because if you did then I would do what you wanted?"

"That's exactly what I'm saying, Xi." He moved forward then and reached out, taking her hand in his. "I have wanted you from the moment I saw you, but you were, ah, you are human, Xi. A shifter would be on more equal ground with me. As you are now, anything we speak of would be unfair."

"All my decisions have been my own so far," she pointed out. "If that were true then how is that possible? We get under each other's skin like it's our job. I have my own," she paused, throwing out her arms as she struggled for the right words, "I have my own agency. My wants are separate from what you want. So how can what you're saying be true?"

He gave her a rueful smile. "That is because all my desires have been aligned with giving you exactly what you want. It hasn't been easy. I have fought myself on more than one night when all I cared to do was pull you close and claim you."

Her mouth dropped open. "You can't be freaking serious."

"I am."

"Hell."

He laughed, and looked back over his shoulder. "Speaking of hell..." Ximena crossed her arms when his voice trailed off.

"What do you mean? Why are you looking at your scribbles like that?"

"Sigils and runes, arcane magic. Not scribbles, Xi." He let out a sigh that made her think of the put upon dowager duchess in her favorite web series. She stuck her tongue out at him and flicked a hand in the air.

"Whatever, Blue. When you're doing a big reveal, you don't just trail off at 'hell.' It's rude."

"That's what's related to hell." He pointed up at the ceiling when the wards went off again. She wondered how long they were going to hold before whatever the hell was trying to get in managed to do it.

She joined him in looking up at the ceiling. "How long are those going to--"

"A demon attacked me outside," he said, and she snapped her attention back to him so fast she nearly gave herself whiplash.

"Sorry, what?"

"A demon. I think the feral humans summoned it," he said, still looking up at the ceiling in a calm as you please way. As if he hadn't just announced a demon had been summoned.

A. Demon. Had. Been. Summoned.

And yet her mate was nonchalant about the whole damn thing. How he was doing it, she didn't know. Or maybe she did. He was a fairy. Of course a fairy wouldn't blink at getting attacked and nearly bleeding out by way of demon. She sucked in a breath at his words, and Blue looked at her in concern.

"Are you all right?" he asked.

"No. Noooooo," she said stretching out the word and shaking her head for emphasis. "And hell no! I am not all right. What do you mean 'a demon was summoned'."

"By feral humans. Don't leave out that part."

"Right now the feral humans are pretty pedestrian in comparison to a goddamn demon, Blue."

He pursed his lips and then gave her a nod. "Fair point."

"So get to explaining why you were scribbling in the dirt when we have a demon trying to break in."

He scoffed at her and took a step back towards the closet. "As I said before, it's runes and sigils, not scribbling, Xi." She followed him involuntarily, her feet carrying her closer to her mate—if there was a demon, she wanted to be near the fairy. It didn't matter if he and his dirt drawings could do anything, or not. She just didn't want to be alone if a demon with a breaking and entering fixation managed to cross Blue's wards. She came to a stop behind Blue's once again crouching form.

"What are you doing?" she asked, leaning forward to peek over his shoulder. She could see what looked like….she tilted her head to the side taking in the chicken scratch on the ground and shook her head. She had no clue what the hell she was looking at.

"Putting out a little summoning call of our own," he replied. He paused and considered the markings before he reached forward and added a final line. "There it's done." Blue stood then and turned towards her with a reassuring smile but why he thought she would be reassured by this, she didn't know.

Ximena cleared her throat, holding one finger up and asked, "Okayyyyy, but fill a girl in on the details? I have no clue what you mean by--"

A flash of light exploded overhead and Ximena screamed in surprise as glitter rained down around them. "What the hell is that?" she cried, jumping behind Blue. She blinked hard, trying to focus on whoever or whatever had just caused the giant glitter light show in their basement, but all she could see were vague outlines. She reached out, her hand smacking against Blue's arm. Her fingers tightened on his bicep when he flexed.

"What are you doing?" she hissed, hating that she couldn't see but still had the presence of mind, or lust, to feel up her mate.

"Showing off?" Blue flexed again and laughed when she didn't let go of his bicep. Instead she leaned in and let her forehead hit his shoulder with a sigh.

"What's with the glitter bomb?" she opted for when she realized she was fighting a losing battle with her hands and their hungry little journey. Her priorities were not in step with the current situation of demon summoning and whatever Blue had called for via dirt scribbles.

"Ah, that," he nodded and then reaching back wrapped an arm around her shoulders and brought her in front of him. "That," he said, leaning down to speak in her ear when he had her leaning back against him, an arm around her waist, "is my mother."

"Your what?" she gasped with a jerk in his hold. She had just begun to enjoy being held this close to him when he dropped the M word.

"My mother."

"You called your mother?" She paused, giving him an incredulous look, and then added, "With dirt scribbles?"

"Those are runes, darling." A voice came from the still cascading glitter and Ximena's head swiveled back to see that from the glitter shower and subsiding light a fairy was stepping forward with the confident stride she had only seen from a pageant queen on one of those reality shows she had taken to watching with Blue.

"Holy shit," Ximena whispered, her eyes going wide when she realized the fairy was, well, big. As in, her wings were big and beautiful. Lilac, smooth and strong, Ximena could easily imagine the fairy taking to the sky with equal parts speed and strength. She had the same cerulean skin as Blue. She could see the resemblance in their features at first blush, the light hued hair that reminded her of moonbeams, the uncanny way their smiles seemed to be the same shape. She might not have noticed that, if it weren't for how much she loved Blue's genuine smiles. And the fairy was giving her one hell of a bright toothy grin that hinted at sharp canines.

Somehow, in this setting, it seemed only welcoming. She had been warned not to trust fairies, and maybe even now she was making a mistake in thinking the smile friendly, but she didn't much care. Not with Blue's arm around her waist, lips close to her ear telling her this was his mother.

She could trust her mate's mother...right?

"Hello there, Ximena," the fairy lifted a hand to her chest and gave a slight bow. "I am Althea, the fairy queen. But you..." she paused and gave her a little wink, "may simply call me mother. Or Al. I like Al as well."

"What?" Ximena felt like the world was falling out from under her. "You're a queen?"

"I am."

Ximena raised a hand that was now shaking from the sudden rush of fear that had fallen upon her at Althea's introduction. "But that means--that means that--"

Althea pursed her lips and finished the sentence that seemed to be stuck in Ximena's throat, and on her lips. "Yes, my dear, that means you're human because of me."

"You took away our powers. I—my powers," Ximena managed to choke out.

"You were very naughty children." Althea shook a finger at her.

"I didn't do it!"

The fairy queen paused, and then nodded. "No, you did not."

"But I'm still stuck this way all the same, and I-I don't know the first thing about being human."

Althea sighed and crossed her arms, giving her son a disapproving look. "All this time with your mate and I can sniff out you haven't bonded one bit! To add insult to injury, you haven't given her the confidence to move in the human world?"

"I have been trying, but she hasn't taken to it as I hoped."

Althea rubbed at her temples with a grimace. "Princes are all the same. You lazy, pretty things. Even after a thousand years, you haven't changed."

Ximena's mouth dropped open. A thousand years. Her mate was how old?

Blue's arm tightened around her waist and he placed a hand on her shoulder, pulling her more securely against him as he leaned over it to speak to his mother.

"I'm sorry, but do you even know the first thing about life without magic? It isn't exactly something that has ever been done before. I am the first fairy to attempt it in five hundred years, and we all know how the previous attempt went. There's the internet now. Do you even know what the internet is?"

Ximena's attention bounced from Blue to his

mother. It was like watching a tennis match of the finest talent. "Wait, time out. How did that go?" she asked, wanting to know what the hell had happened five hundred years ago. Why did Blue sound so annoyed about it? Whatever it was, it couldn't have been good.

"I know. I told you this when you chose her," Althea reminded him, tapping at her chin and ignoring Ximena's question. Though when she saw the fairy queen's eyes on her she knew she had heard her, she was simply choosing not to answer. "You knew the challenges ahead of you."

Ximena felt him stiffen at her back but then he breathed out a long sigh and she felt him drop his chin until it was tucked against her neck. He breathed in deeply then, the exhale of it tickling her skin in a way that nearly made her gasp. Might have almost made her moan in pleasure and tip her head back, offering him her neck by instinct. Hell, she might have done it if his mother wasn't in the same room and, you know, a fairy freaking queen. Ximena bit back her sudden need to turn to a pile of goo in her mate's arms and forced herself to think of the least sexy thing imaginable. Pencil lead, empty ketchup bottles, doing what she heard was a thing called taxes.

Oh, there it was.

Her desire for him dried up in the face of filing taxes and securing a driving permit. Nothing like a little paperwork to tamp down lusty need.

"I did," Blue murmured, lips grazing her skin. He

lifted his head and looked at his mother then. "And I would choose it all over again, day after day, hour after hour, if it meant that she would be mine. Human or not."

Althea considered them. Her black eyes slowly moved over them as the wards screamed overhead--- an event that was not truly a pressing matter when her mate's mother was looking them over like they were a complicated problem she could not solve.

"I had not seen this," she said softly. "I had thought…" her voice trailed off and she huffed out a laugh, one that was bitter and quick to end. "I had thought you would give it up when she did not come to you. When her fear got the best of her, and then…well. Then you would be lost to one another."

Ximena felt her stomach drop to her feet. The fairy queen had not only taken her ability to shift, but she had also nearly taken her mate from her. She had known that she would be afraid, that her worry and anxiety would keep her from Blue. What was more, she had anticipated Ximena would not take the risk on Blue. That she would lose her mate.

She felt as if her chest might burst from the sudden surge of rage that flooded her. She had been fighting her pull to Blue, forcing herself to think of a tomorrow without him in it. And his mother had known all the while.

Althea pursed her lips, wings fluttering behind her. "And yet, here we are."

"Yes, here we fucking are," Ximena bit out, not

caring that cursing at your mate's mother was not advisable behavior. Even without them having fairy queen status. That little addition just added on to the inadvisable nature, she supposed. But hey, whatever. She didn't really care if she got zapped into a bug at this point, because she was ticked.

A normal mate might have warned her against picking a fight with the fairy queen, but Ximena's? Well, he just chuckled and kissed her cheek while she faced off with his mother. Her skin tingled from the brush of his lips, but she refused to become distracted by fairy man kisses! She was going to give Althea a piece of her mind.

"Are you angry then?" Althea asked, crossing her arms. She took a step closer and her wings unfurled to their full width, filling the basement with beauty and wonder. How kickass were her wings? But no, Ximena gave herself a mental shake. Must not become infatuated with fairy mother's wings. She had to remain strong.

"Yes, I'm," she drew herself up and brought both of her hands together in front of her, palm-to-palm, pressing them back against her chest as she drew in a calming breath, *"angry.* How else would I feel? You took my wolf from me. You knew I would mess this up between us, and you stayed silent on it! You didn't want us together, did you?"

"No." It was succinct, but honest.

"But why?" Ximena whispered. "After all the pain I

went through with the Bloodstones, as a wolf that you had a hand in making, why?"

"Blue would, in the end, give up his fairy nature for you."

"I would never ask him to do that!"

"And he would refuse to live without you. Even if you were a shifter, you would not live a millennia, not even half. But he will."

Ximena jerked back as if she had been slapped. In all her thoughts of a life without Blue, she had never once considered her life span.

"Oh no," she whispered, but Blue was there shaking his head and squeezing her to him once more.

"I don't care. I would make this choice again and again and again. All the best people are...well, people," he said.

"You can't do it."

"Xi, it's already done. Why do you think I couldn't fight the demon?" he asked, and she went stock still. She hadn't thought of that.

"But you healed, upstairs…"

"A little gift left over from my time as a fairy prince. I'll always heal fast. Our children will have a bit of that as well."

"Our children?"

He leaned close, cheek to hers, and she felt him smile. "It's a thought. We can also adopt an ungodly amount of dogs, too. Either way, I'll be happy if you're with me, Xi."

She raised her hands and rested them on the arm

that was curled around her and laughed, feeling her eyes sting with tears. She hated crying in front of the fairy queen. Yeah, she was still pretty pissed at her, but there was no getting away from the emotion Blue's words had inspired in her. So she cried and squeezed his arm.

"I think I love you."

"Does that mean you've forgiven me?" Althea wanted to know. Ximena glared at the fairy queen.

"No, I'm still mad."

"I don't blame you. It was unkind of me to let you both flounder here in the human world."

"It's not so bad. There's pizza," Blue interjected and his mother gave him a raised eyebrow.

"Is pizza really worth you lingering in that human form of yours? I have no idea how you stand it."

He shrugged. "Drives Xi wild. Seems worth all the walking. Besides, it's not like I can change back now, can I?"

Both Althea and Ximena blew out a long suffering synchronized sigh. "Men."

A crash overhead made them all pause. The trio lifted their gaze to the ceiling as the sound of glass hitting the floor and heavy footsteps above them signaled they were no longer alone in the house.

"Seems the wards finally gave," Blue muttered with a tsk. He let go of Ximena then and she hated that she instantly wanted to reach for him. She managed to keep herself in check, but only just. He pointed above them and said, "That's why I summoned you. I told you

I wouldn't come back without my mate, and I've got her. But those little pups you set loose in the woods have done a very bad thing."

The sound of smashing china and what could only be the kitchen table Ximena loved being overturned above them made her wince. There was not going to be any going back to their home, not after whatever was up there was done with it.

"And a very loud thing," Althea observed. A bang and then more heavy, slow footsteps that set off in the other direction of the house, to the living room, began and she sighed. "Very big as well, I'd say."

"It's a demon," Blue told her as he rubbed his jaw. "At least I think it is. I wasn't sure, not from where it got me."

Althea shook her head and reached out to touch his still bloodied shirt. "You really must keep a more careful eye."

"It was dark."

"You were a fairy. You know better. You were sloppy."

"Can you two stop arguing? We have to stop whatever that is," Ximena gestured towards the basement door where a thump was heard. Their guest had zeroed in on their location in the basement, because in the next second the door was ripped off its hinges and a low growl was heard.

"Shit," Ximena breathed. "Double shit."

It stepped onto the first step, and then the next, and then it was barreling down the staircase towards them.

Ximena turned and threw herself in front of Blue. She was human, yes, so her doing so was pretty stupid given that she couldn't defend herself, but she'd just found him, just given herself permission to want him.

She couldn't lose him like this. She couldn't not try.

And so she stepped forward trying to throw him behind her, but it seemed Blue was of the same opinion, and the pair collided in a tangle of arms and legs. They tripped and hit the ground with a groan and a thud while Althea rolled her eyes at them.

"Mates really are rendered entirely useless aren't they?" she asked, stepping over them and holding out her hand towards the thing. And 'thing' was the only way to describe what was before them, given that it was just a shadow really. It was an absence of light and movement but somehow it was made solid, and it was huge. The only thing Ximena caught sight of were teeth. Sharp, nearly rotting and yellowed teeth that snapped and would, if given the chance, rip them apart. Claws dug into the wood splintering it with each bound of the demon careening towards them.

Ximena lay there face half in the dirt and under Blue, her mate's legs by her head. How that happened she wasn't quite sure. They hadn't exactly been graceful in their urgency to save each other. If she had known this was how they were going to meet the demon she might have left her telling off of Althea for a later time, but *c'est la vie*.

Just two newly made humans lying ass up in the dirt, waiting for a giant shadow demon to eat them.

Or, that might have been the case, except that all it took was a dainty flick of Althea's wrist to stop it. Light from her fingers filled the demon's form until it was glowing so brightly it rivaled the fairy queen's disco ball entrance.

It froze, and for a second it was actually kind of pretty.

Until it exploded.

CHAPTER SIX

Whence shadow demon beasts exploded, you might think they would just quietly evaporate. That wasn't the case.

Not even a little bit.

When shadow demon beasts got their asses handed to them by a fairy, they exploded all right, but they did so like any living thing. That meant guts, blood, and bone. Then there were those terrifying teeth Ximena had thought were going to rip her and her mate apart. All of that meant a big clean up, because walking around with demon guts in your hair was frowned upon in any establishment, or dimension it seemed. Which was why they were now standing in front of a fairy bathhouse covered head-to-toe in demon guts and getting dirty looks from the fairies around them.

"It's not like we planned this," Ximena told one Fey woman who got too close and wrinkled her nose. Blue chuckled and tossed an arm over her shoulder, dragging her close.

"Ignore the judgey looks. A lot of the Fey can be uptight on account of not mingling with the other supernaturals."

"And now we're human," she reminded him.

He paused and pushed out his lips, thinking on it. "Yeah, we aren't even supernaturals. Is there a subcategory for ex-supernatural?" He turned then and looked at his mother who had materialized back beside him.

Althea shook her head. "Can't say that I've had a demand for such a thing."

"Who knows, I might start a trend."

"Good heavens I hope not." Althea frowned and then gestured to the attendant at the desk. "See that these two filthy fools are cleaned head-to-toe," she glanced back at them and then said, "it may take all day, but see that it happens. And feed them too before you have them brought to my home."

"As you will, my Queen."

Ximena raised her eyebrows at Blue and mouthed "My Queen" to which he laughed and grabbed her hand. "Come on, Xi. You haven't lived until you've experienced a fairy bath house."

"What's that supposed to mean?"

He grinned and waved goodbye to his mother as they were led towards two floor-to-ceiling pearlesque doors covered in delicate gold filigree.

"You'll see, Xi. Best not to spoil the surprise."

"Have fun and make wise choices! Oh, and remember, do not drink the wine!" Althea called after them. Those first parting words all seemed to track for a mother sending her son and his mate off to the spa, but those last ones….Ximena turned back towards her and opened her mouth to ask what the hell she meant, but it was too late. The fairy queen was gone, and she was being ushered forward by another too pretty fairy, this one with pink wings of gossamer and hair that looked like spun gold.

"You want to explain what mommy-dearest meant by 'don't drink the wine?'" she asked, looking behind her still. "I mean, I like wine. Or at least, I think I do…" She hadn't had wine before, she'd had mead and beer on a rare occasion with the Bloodstones. Since she'd left with Blue she hadn't really thought about it, and he'd never made mention of it. However, now that she was being told not to…

"You should not take the bait from her. She knows you're going to want to drink it," Blue advised her. They walked through the doors and she might have protested that she wasn't taking the bait; she was asserting herself as a modern woman in a world of fairies and demons that went kaboom all over her and got stuck in her hair. She frowned and flicked a piece of demon from her hair onto the floor. A passing fairy gasped and leapt back from the demon splatter.

Ximena winced, offering them a weak, "Sorry," on her way past.

"Oh come off it, Belinda. We all know what you got into at the last Beltane. I see you." Two of Blue's fingers came up, flicking from his eyes to the now red faced fairy. Ximena clapped a hand over her mouth to stifle a laugh at the embarrassed fairy hurrying away while Blue glared at her.

"What's Beltane?" she asked him. "Is that some kind of fairy holiday..." her voice trailed off when she turned and took in the entirety of the fairy spa. If heaven were invaded by insanely good looking models of varying supernatural predilection, then this was what she imagined heaven to look like. The room's ceilings extended high up, far higher than she could see with bright light streaming down from above. The walls were made of teal tile, with plants climbing them, making her think of a forest.

Crystal steaming pools of water dotted the room. Fairies relaxed in them, their perfect bodies on display for all to see. The Fey were not held back by such things as clothing or silly human ideas of modesty. No, this was a natural as you please place, with more naked flesh than she had ever seen in her entire life-and she had been a wolf.

Wolves weren't exactly known for modesty, but they came by it honestly. The Fey seemed to relish it. Chaise lounges and piles of soft looking pillows and blankets served as spots of respite for lounging fairies.

"Where the hell are we?" she whispered, moving closer to his side.

"The spa," Blue answered simply, looking at her in surprise for a moment before he grinned and tilted his head looking back out at the fairies. Suddenly his eyes cut to her. "Oh, I see what you're hung up on."

"I'm not hung up on anything," she insisted.

"Aren't you though?" His hand moved to the small of her back. They were following the fairy put in charge of them at a decent pace, and she nearly tripped over a leg she hadn't noticed in front of her. She had only managed to right herself when she nearly stumbled again at a moan to the left. She jumped in surprise, barely managing to keep herself on her feet. Blue hooked an arm around her waist but she skipped away from him.

"I'm fine, I'm fine, there's absolutely nothing that would make me nervous around here, okay? I'm cool as a cucumber," she told him over her shoulder, pretending not to notice the knowing look on Blue's handsome face. She wrapped her arms around her waist. She was suddenly unsure of what to do with herself, her limbs were...awkward. Too long, too uncoordinated and her skin. Goddess, her skin was practically burning up, prickly and too tight. She hadn't felt this way since she was a shifter. Why was she feeling it now? The only time she had been overcome by this light in the head and tight in the chest feeling was before the full moon shift, when she'd always felt out of control.

She took in a shallow breath. That was it. Out of control. All around her sighs and giggles were rising as surely as the steam. It was hard not to feel out of control or...light in the head. Any woman would react this way, and in her entirely human state she was no exception.

"Are you sure about that? You're blushing."

"You aren't even looking at me. How do you know I'm blushing?" she wanted to know as she kept marching forward, doing her damndest to keep her eyes on the back of the fairy guiding them to wherever the hell they were going, as an all out pleasure party was in full swing around her. Was this what the spa was like in the human world? She bit her lip and considered it. She didn't think she'd mind that.

Blue's hand on her shoulder made her jump in surprise, but she refused to look at him. "Hands off, fairy man."

"It's just man now. Not a fairy anymore, Xi."

She frowned and looked at him then. She had forgotten Blue had given up his, well,...fairyness for her. For the sake of their mate bond. Except, that now if he was human...didn't that mean...*that...*

"If you're human, then are we mates?"

Ahead of them the fairy leading them paused to glance back at them. She was standing in front of a set of large hammered silver doors. These ones were inset with colored glass radiating with a light from within. Shades of purple, pink and turquoise light shone on the floor and moved over their faces and bodies as they came to a stop in front of the doors.

The fairy cleared her throat and Ximena knew she had heard her question Blue, but rather than linger she simply inclined her head and pressed a hand to the door.

"Your bath awaits you inside. Food and drink as well." A click from the door sounded as it popped open an inch beneath her palm. "If you require anything more, you know how to send for us." This was directed at Blue and then just like that the golden hair fairy was turning on her heel and making her way back down the hallway in that floating-too-graceful-for-human-eyes way the Fey had about them.

When they were alone Ximena held up a finger and made to repeat her question, but Blue waved a hand at her and pulled open the door.

"Inside, Xi. We can talk inside."

Her lips pressed into a thin line at that but she gave him a quick nod and stepped inside. She could wait a minute more to get answers to the questions now spinning through her mind at warp speed. Though when she stepped into the center of the room and took a minute to look around it was hard to keep focused on exactly what questions she had that required attention.

The room was in a word: sensational.

It was a mini version of the common area they had walked through. There was a decadent feast laid out on a low sitting table. She glimpsed more food than she could, or had, ever eaten all on golden plates, bottles of sparkly glowing liquid on one side of it. The wine she had been warned to drink. She took a hesitant step towards the sparkling drink, but stopped quickly when she remembered Blue's advice to ignore his mother.

She felt drawn to the bottles. Felt like she had to pick it up, uncork one and pour its contents into one of the golden cups at the table. It would be sweet, she knew it. Ximena could nearly taste it on her tongue, and when she closed her eyes she thought of summer and strawberries, of the way sunshine warmed your skin.

Light, sweet, and warm. It smelled like Blue to her.

She opened her eyes in confusion. How could she still scent him when he was human? Her eyes swept the room as if she could find clues in it if she searched hard enough. Pale teal tiles shot through with veins of gold made up the walls and floors, a pool of swirling water in what looked to be... moonstone? Ximena recognized the rock, as it was one shifters, wolves in particular, favored for its connection to the moon, and by proxy their primal side. She'd had a small piece she had carried with her, a prized possession when she was a Bloodstone. So little had been pretty when she lived with her once pack. She used to carry that piece of Moonstone in her palm, hand clamped tightly around it until her fingers ached from the pressure of it.

She'd sworn she would find more than a little pretty in her life. That she would find beautiful. And now, here it was in the form of a large gleaming pool of moonstone that glowed so brightly she realized it was the source of the light that had shone through the colored glass on the door.

Beautiful was not just this room though, Ximena

realized, turning to look at her mate. It was having Blue at her side.

Blue was as he had always been to her.

Beautiful.

But that still left one question, the question she had tried to ask him before.

"You're human now but humans don't have mates. Why would you give up your life as a fairy for me?"

He smiled at her and closed the door with his shoulder. "I don't care if humans don't have mates. We are, Xi."

"But there's nothing keeping us together," she whispered, voice cracking.

"That's where you're wrong, Xi. There is something greater than all the magic and fate combined in this world or the next, that is keeping us together." He pushed away from the door and came forward. Ximena ignored the pull of the bottles and met him halfway until they were toe-to-toe at the center of the room. The gentle sound of the bubbling moonstone pool the only sound in the room save for their breathing.

"What is that?" she asked, taking the bait when Blue looked content to wait on her. He lifted a hand and caught a lock of her hair, curling it around his finger. He did that for a second, watching the dark hair tighten around his finger before he let it go and raised his eyes to hers.

When he did, she saw that it was the same lavender hued eyes she had fallen for all those weeks ago. Had continued to fall for a little more each day, even as she fought it. It never mattered if Blue was in his fairy form, or human form as he was now and would be from now on, Ximena had fallen for him, and she had fallen hard.

She loved him. And mating bond or not, he was the one she had come to love.

"Choice," he told her, eyes moving slowly over her face. He raised a hand to cup her cheek and tilt her head back to look at him. "Choice is what keeps us together. It isn't a bond, or biology, or some game my mother played with her fairy court to decide our fate. It's you and I choosing one another every day from here on out that matters, Xi."

She smiled. The words were tender and true. She knew her mate meant them. Ximena liked to think of Blue as her mate, even if there was no more magic between them. It still felt right.

"I choose you," she whispered, wrapping an arm around his neck and leaning into him. "I choose you, Blue. Now and tomorrow."

He pulled her close then, a hand pressed flat to her back, bringing her into his chest. The hand at her cheek splayed out to cradle her face as their lips met in a kiss.

Oh, that *kiss.*

Ximena felt as if she were having life, and breath, and goddess...every good thing she had ever known or ever hoped to know poured right into her from that first brush of lips. It was tender and sweet---the way she had thought a kiss with a mate should be. This was the kiss she would remember, not the one with him covered in blood while fear overtook her.

No, this was one of wanting and gentleness. Lips and tongues moving together slowly in an exploration that was unhurried.

They could take their time here. They were safe here and could fully and finally enjoy the other as they pleased. She reached for him with her free hand, fingers finding their way beneath his shirt and she nearly moaned into his mouth at the first brush of her fingers against his skin. Another moment went by and she became braver, fingers giving way to the press of her palm against his muscled stomach. Blue drew back and looked down at her, his eyes hungry, and she knew he didn't give a damn about the feast in the room. He was looking at her as if she were the feast and she smiled up at him, enjoying the knowledge that her mate wanted her—no, needed her, and desperately so.

"Ximena, I need you." Blue's chest was rising and falling, his breathing coming fast and quick and Ximena knew hers was doing the same. Their kiss may have been gentle and all the softness they needed together after their encounter with the demon, but it was the match that lit the tinder of their desire. That small spark was now a full blaze that demanded them to touch and kiss, caress every inch of the other. Without hesitation Ximena reached for her shirt and yanked it over her head.

"Then have me," she told him. Blue looked down at her, the hunger unmistakable in his stare but then she saw his lips twitch up into a smile. This fairy was up to something, and right in the middle of what was supposed to be a pretty sexy time. "What is it?" she asked.

"I'm working out the best way to get the demon guts off of us." He reached out and flicked off a piece of what could only be said 'demon guts.' Ximena winced, remembering that yes, they were covered in an exploded demon. She blamed the fairy orgy they had walked through and whatever was in the moonstone pool. Also whatever the hell was swirling around so invitingly in the bottles lining the table. She glanced their way, attention diverted for a moment, before she shook herself and forced her eyes back to Blue's.

Why she was so fixated on those wine bottles was not the pressing issue. Getting clean, and then dirty again, most preferably with Blue, was what mattered.

"The pool," she said, pointing a finger at the water and beginning to unbutton her jeans. "Get in the water. It's moonstone and we both know that means we'll be clean in no time."

Blue hummed in agreement. "It is fortunate we have a moonstone bath. No other way to get this kind of darkness off." He pulled off his shirt, and before Ximena could even manage to get her pants past her thighs he had also kicked his shoes, pants and underwear, to the side.

"How are you that fast?" she wondered out loud when he was standing at the moonstone pool's edge. She wouldn't complain about how quick he was, not when she was afforded an amazing view of his ass, which was pretty incredible but also making her feel like she was having an out of body experience. She'd gone from a first kiss to now getting an eyeful of wonderfully toned ass. In fact, every inch of Blue was wonderfully toned, his body was lean and muscular in a way that reminded her of the easy grace she had always known Blue to move with.

His broad shoulders moved and she bit her lip, watching his back muscles bunch and coil. Then there was his ass. She couldn't stop looking at that ass. The man had an incredible one.

"Hey, my eyes are up here, Xi." Blue waved a hand at her and she flushed.

"Not my fault, when you have that junk in the trunk."

He laughed. "We are going to have to update your slang. Even I know that's old." He turned back to the moonstone pool and stepped down into it with a sigh. "Now come over here and join me, hmm?"

She nodded. "Yeah, okay." Ximena kept undressing, her eyes on Blue the entire time as he moved further back into the pool until the water was up to his chest. She dropped her bra to the side and watched with a thrill of pleasure as he bit his lip, eyes moving over her bare breasts.

There was a power in watching the man she wanted want her just as desperately. She smiled at him and reached for her panties, fingers hooking under the waistband of them. She didn't miss the way his breath hitched. He was leaning back against the moonstone's wall, arms extended on either side bracing him against the wall as he watched her. Slowly she lowered her panties, an inch, and then another, and then another until she was right above the part of her she knew he wanted to see the most. She paused, fingers pressing down against her thighs and then blew out a breath as she pushed the panties down her legs and stepped out of them.

"You're beautiful," Blue told her. And when he looked at her the way he was, she believed him. He was drinking her up as surely as any thirsty man in a desert would.

"Even covered in demon guts?" she asked with a grin.

"Oh, especially covered in demon guts. I'd have you no other way, Xi." He leaned forward and held out a hand to her. He didn't ask for her to come to him, he didn't need to. There wasn't a part of Ximena that didn't want to go to him, and so she walked forward on shaking legs until she was stepping down into the moonstone pool.

She gasped when her feet hit the water. The pool was gently sloping, the water rising with each step until it was at her waist and she was in front of Blue. "I wasn't expecting that," she told him, and took another step towards him. There was an electric current in the water, or what she thought that would feel like. Effervescent bubbles tickled her skin and in its wake, a refreshing feeling settled in, making her muscles relax.

She felt like she could float away. She might have tried it, if Blue hadn't reached for her.

"You have beautiful hair," he said, fingers carding through her dark tresses. "I've always loved your hair."

"I like your hair too."

"Thank you. It has demon guts in it and so does yours. Let's get it clean and then I can appreciate it to the fullest extent." She laughed and nodded, turning so that her back was to him. "Tip your head back," Blue said, gently tilting her head back. Ximena leaned into his touch, following his direction, and sighed happily when he began to pour water over her head. She almost asked where he got the pitcher he was currently using, but in the fairy realm who knew?

It could have come from anywhere really, and who cared at this point? All she wanted to do was close her eyes and let Blue take care of her.

So she did exactly just that.

⊱✾⊰

It seemed a moonstone pool did make fairly quick work of cleaning up any remaining bad vibes and guts left behind by a demon attacker, and the pair were soon as clean as they ever hoped to be. The waters of the pool were also pristine. Ximena supposed it was the purifying powers of the stone, plus whatever fairy magic that gave the waters their ability to stay pure. She smiled and moved a hand across the water, her fingertips dragging across the surface of it. It was a beautiful place really. She was so happy to be there with Blue. She looked up at him and bit her lip when she saw him staring at her in a way that she knew had nothing to do with telling her if her hair was finally clean, or not.

This man wanted exactly what she did. To touch and be touched.

"We're clean now," she said.

"So we are," he agreed.

"Well, I guess that means we can get to it then."

"And what's 'it'?" Blue asked.

"The touching," she flicked a finger between the two of them, water droplets flying from her hand. "We are going to touch now, right?" Goddess, she hoped they were going to.

He moved then with that too easy speed he had retained somehow, and before she could blink she was in his arms.

"Oh, yeah, we are going to touch." His hands moved then, slipping across her wet skin. She shivered, leaning into him. She wanted his hands all over her, wanted him in every way she could get. Wanted all of him.

"I've only done this a few times, and all of those times I didn't enjoy it all that much," she explained. The shifters in her pack weren't known for their gentleness, neither had what they had shared together been tender. It had been about fulfilling a need, an urge in them both, *but this?*

This was different for Ximena.

There was nothing she didn't want from Blue. Nothing she didn't want to give him either, and all of it was achingly sweet...even if she wanted more than sweet him. She wanted it all. "But I think—I *know* I'll like it with you."

Blue kissed her, his mouth slanting just right to hers. He took his time in tasting her mouth and lips, leaving her breathing hard and more than sure she was going to like whatever touching was about to go down. "Oh, you will, and if you don't then tell me and we will keep trying until we find something you *do* like. Whatever you want, Xi."

She groaned at that and then shook her head. "All I want is you," she said, wrapping her arms around him and pressing her water slick body close to his. "You're what I want."

"Aren't we lucky, then?" He kissed her again but this time it was her chin and then her jaw. He had a handful of her hair and he tipped her head back, and tugged. The suddenness of it made her moan. "I plan on making you a very happy woman." He turned them until she was back against the pool wall and slipped a hand between them. She arched her back when she felt his palm skim across her stomach before his fingers were venturing lower, until she felt the ghost of his touch across the lips of her pussy.

"I'm already happy," she told him through a breathless sigh.

"Then happier. Ecstatic. Overjoyed." Each word was punctuated by another stroke of his thumb across her clit. His fingers were tracing the outline of her and she opened her legs to him, one on either side as he stepped in closer until he was nestled between her thighs. "Maybe even pleasantly pleased?" He kissed her again, lips moving across her skin lightly before she felt the flick of his tongue. It was a light touch but when she dropped her head back, giving him her neck, Blue groaned. The light brush of his tongue became more than that. He licked his way down her throat, the movement of his tongue matching the thrusting of his fingers moving in and out of her now.

"Yes. Pleasantly pleased." Her hips moved in time with his fingers. To call herself pleasantly pleased was an understatement. A ball of pleasure was slowly growing in her belly, the warmth of it moving over her limbs as surely as the water did. Where she had once felt soothed and restored by the pool, Blue's touch was now replacing it with a heat she had only encountered before her shift at the full moon. Even in the warm water her body trembled, and goosebumps formed across her skin. It made her shiver and reach for Blue then. He jerked his head up and away from her neck to take her mouth in a hungry kiss. Her tongue met his and she gasped, the sound of it swallowed by Blue's answering moan. He increased the pressure of his thumb against her clit and the gentle warmth that had been overtaking her was replaced by a fever pitch of pleasure that she was powerless to escape, tipping right over and into.

"Blue, Blue!" she cried out, arms clenching around

her mate as she orgasmed. The suddenness of it surprised her, leaving her breathless and shaking. Her fingers dug into his flesh, the hard muscle of him beneath her fingertips would no doubt be bruised from it, but she couldn't force herself to let go. Everything her mate was, this man that was bound to her not by biology or magic, but choice, made every part of her desire to cling to him with both hands.

"Blue," she whispered, and this time the word was a promise. They both heard it with Blue kissing her cheek, his fingers still gently stroking her, coaxing her down from her orgasm in a way that was encouraging her to climb that mountain one more time. She opened her eyes and looked up at him, raising a leg to hook around his waist.

"Have me," she told me.

"Goddess, yes," Blue groaned, reaching down to grab her thigh. He pulled her tight to him, lifting her legs until both were wrapped around him and lined himself up to her. The head of his cock made her thighs clench in anticipation and then he was thrusting forward and sinking into her with a satisfied sigh.

"You are so beautiful," he told her, as he began to slowly move inside of her. The hard length of his cock was beyond perfect. Ximena brought herself close, both arms wrapped around his neck, her cheek pressed to his as their bodies began to slowly move in tandem.

"So are you," she whispered back through a smile. The drag of his cock against her when he pulled all the way out and thrust forward, filling her entirely, had her crying out. She might have told him that he was a master at teasing, that he knew exactly what he was doing taking it this slow with her, but she enjoyed the slow build between them. But she didn't quite have it in her to form actual words beyond *'Blue,' 'more,' and 'yes.'*

Blue turned them so that his back was braced against the wall, his hands at her hips. Ximena put her hands out, palms flat against the cool tile of the floor. She pushed on it, using it for leverage as their movements lost their almost lazy rhythm for a quicker pace that punched the breath right out of her.

"Xi, goddess, Xi!" Blue's hands tightened on her waist. He was grinding his hips up into her, the water sloshing between them with every thrust, and she leaned forward, claiming his mouth in a kiss. She was going to come again. Just another few strokes. The push of his pelvis slanting against hers drove her closer, and then after one more thrust between them there it was. She came with a shout, her mouth against Blue's as she clenched around him. The pressure of it was enough to bring him with her. She felt him spasm, body clenching, muscles bunching and coiling under her hands and against her body.

They held each other when they both came down from their high, both taking in shuddering and gasping breaths as they clung to one another. Water swirled around them, the glow of the moonstone pool making Ximena think that this must be what it would be like to be on the moon. You know, if the moon was populated by men bent on bringing you pleasure while you floated in pure starlight.

If the moon was, then she would move there immediately. As soon as there was air to breath she would move there, but for now this would more than do. She smiled at him, her heart racing when Blue returned the gesture.

"That was amazing," she said finally when they had both caught their breath.

"Amazing is putting it mildly." Blue grinned at her and slowly let her go. Hands leaving her waist as she slid down from her perch in his arms. She laughed and splashed water at him.

"Not bad for a couple of humans, huh? If they keep talking about how sex with mates is so much better, and that's what we did as humans, then I'm starting to wonder what the shifters are doing when they aren't with their mate."

Blue barked out a laugh and leaned his head back, wetting his hair in the water. He sank down then dunking himself full, and when he reemerged he was beside her. "You know there might be something to that, but trust me…." He was leaning down to look at her until their lips were only an inch from the other. "Fairies know how to fuck," he informed her.

Her lips parted, a laugh husking out between them and she grinned at him. "You're right. You do, even if you aren't a fairy anymore." His eyes went dark at that and she winced at his expression. "I'm sorry," she offered lamely when she could think of nothing else.

She raised her arms, crossing them over her exposed breasts. The water was bubbling and swirling around them in gentle waves, but was now around their waists where they stood closer to the entrance of the moon-stone pool.

She ducked her head avoiding his eyes. "I'm sorry, Blue. I--"

"Hey, no. Look at me." Blue came forward, fingers gentle on her chin tilting her head back up to look at him. "Never say you're sorry for what happened. I chose this." His fingers tensed slightly. "You know I would choose this. There is no room for sorries between us."

Her shoulders dropped from around her ears and she nodded, knowing he was right. "I'm sorry, that I'm sorry?" she offered, and he grinned.

"Come on, Xi. There's a feast with your name on it."

"I think you mean our names," she corrected. They left the pool with Blue handing her one of the fluffy towels and robes waiting for them. When she had been with the Bloodstones she'd never had much in the way of comfort, and when she lived with Blue she had thought she was in a palace, but this? This was luxury like she had never known, and she was set on enjoying it all. Ximena sighed happily, wiggling her toes in the plush rug around the feast laden table. She wrapped her hair in the towel and sank down onto the pillows next to Blue, who was already working on filling a plate with food for her.

"Eat up," he said, pushing it in front of her. There

were bright and colorful fruits she had never seen before, alongside meat and cheese, pastries that set her mouth to watering. But before she went to dig she paused, her eyes landing on the line of glass bottles filled with swirling glitter.

"What is that?" she asked.

"The wine."

She pointed at the bottles. "I want that."

"You were told not to drink it," he reminded her, but reached for a bottle all the same. He plucked up a golden cup and considered her over it. "Are you sure?" he asked.

"Very." She pushed aside her plate and reached for the cup, making grabby hands at it. "I want the wine."

"Even with the warning?"

"Even, no, *especially* with the warning. What does she know? She thought I was going to turn away from you," she replied. Blue inclined his head and poured her a cup of the bright light wine.

"You aren't wrong on that one. My mother has a nasty way of thinking she knows everything. But every so often she's wrong." He set the filled cup down and nudged it towards her. "More often than not. She's been wrong a fair amount these days."

"Like with my pack, ah, you know," She waved a hand at him and picked the cup up, "with the battle with--"

"The Bloodstones, yes. She was wrong on how far they were willing to go, but she should have known by the way they treated the weakest of them." He reached out, fingers brushing against a tendril of wet hair that had escaped her towel. "How they treated you."

She swallowed hard and pushed back against the memories that threatened to make themselves known. She wouldn't allow that kind of ugly into a space so beautiful as this, not here, not with them. "That's in the past. And you know what they say about dwelling on the past."

"No, what do they say?" he asked.

She bit her lip, hand on the gold cup's stem. "I don't know, I was hoping you did. I never really got a good handle on human sayings," she admitted.

Blue snorted and poured himself a cup of the wine. "Well whatever the saying is, I have an inkling that you only want to drink this wine because you were told not to."

She pursed her lips, cup raised halfway to them and shrugged. "I'm not saying that you're right or that you're wrong, but I am saying that it doesn't help that it was your mother who told me not to drink it. So I guess...in a sense you're right. On that note," she raised her cup to him in cheers and repeated one of the human sayings she did know, "bottoms up."

Blue clinked his glass to hers and the couple raised their glasses and drank together. Ximena's brows knit together at the first sip. She was braced for the worst to come, but when nothing happened she took another drink, this time deeper and then another when still nothing happened. She only lowered her cup when it was over halfway empty and gave Blue a frown.

"What gives?"

He chuckled and shrugged, looking at his cup with a raised eyebrow. "You know, I was wondering the same—" his voice cut off, and the cup fell from his fingers, falling to the floor with a clank.

"Blue?" Ximena reached for him when he fell back onto the pillows, his body contorting and writhing. "Blue!" she threw her cup to the side and pushed through the pillows to his side. Whatever was working on him from the wine hadn't hit her yet, and she growled in annoyance. Of course the fairy queen's warning hadn't really applied to her, but to her son! The sound of pillows ripping beneath her hands was welcome as the burn of anger she felt towards Althea raged through her. When she got her hands on the fairy she was going to regret ever— wait a second.

Ripping pillows? From her hands? Humans didn't have hands capable of ripping pillows apart, and neither did they have throats able to produce the growl filling the room like she was presently doing.

She sat up straight, hands going to her throat and the familiar feel of her growl rumbling beneath her palms made her stop short with a gasp. She was growling. She was ripping pillows.

"What the fuck was in that wine?" she whispered, glancing back at her cup that was on its side, the glittering contents spilling across the table.

"Magic," Blue croaked from where he was still splayed out on the floor. He pushed his hair to the side and sat up, his robe falling open as he did so. Goddess it was hard to stay in the now when he went around looking good enough to eat.

She cleared her throat and forced her mind towards pure thoughts, or at least thoughts as pure as she could manage when there was magic wine making her feel light-headed?

"What do you mean?"

"She gave us our powers back." He held out a hand and wiggled his fingers, a spray of gold falling from them. "I knew it," he said, looking at her.

"You knew what?" Ximena pressed, sitting back on the pillows and doing her best to take stock of her situation. After a moment she felt her wolf, so close to the surface she nearly wept. It was true, she was a shifter again! "Wait, are you telling me that your mother gave us the ability to take back our lives in that bottle of wine, but then--but then told me not to drink it?"

Blue nodded. "That's exactly what I'm saying."

"Your mom and I are going to have a long talk about this."

"You know, I'd pay to see that. Please have a long talk with her about this." He was smiling as he said this, and Ximena felt her lips turn up into a smile at the sight of her mate's grin. She paused then and said, "You're my mate...*again.*"

"Never stopped being one even with," he flicked a hand dismissively and then grabbed a strawberry off the table, "all the humanity getting in the way."

"That's one way of putting it. But what does this mean for us? What are we now?"

"Super charged mates," he answered through a mouthful of fruit holding one out to her for her to take.

She frowned, taking the strawberry in her hand. "What does that mean?" she asked, before lifting it to her lips and taking a bite. She moaned as the sweet berry burst on her tongue.

It was delicious, and now that she thought about it she was starving. She turned then and reached for the plate Blue had made for her. She was busy eating when Blue finally answered her, and it was lucky that her mouth was currently stuffed with food or she might have choked at his answer.

"It means, mate of mine, we learn the ins and outs of you taking the throne."

Ximena coughed and nearly choked, the latter stopped only when he thumped her on the back. She was still gasping for breath when she managed to croak out, "What? The throne?" she spluttered.

"Yes, you will be the new Fey Queen."

CHAPTER SEVEN

When you thought of the Fey Queen you thought of...well, *a fairy.* Not a wolf shifter who could hardly control her wolf. But here they were, and Ximena guessed stranger things had happened. They were standing in the Queen's sitting room, a retinue of fairy guards at the ready, with Blue beside her and looking, as usual, unbothered.

Well, unbothered and very hot. How he managed to do both at the same time was a mystery.

"He's right. You will succeed me."

"But you told me not to drink the wine."

Althea shrugged and lifted her own cup of wine, taking a dainty sip. "Queens are daring," she said, giving her a smile that made Ximena wary. It was far too much a showing of teeth than a genuine smile, but the Queen was playing nice, so Ximena supposed she could do the same.

For now.

"And Queens don't much enjoy being told what to do, which made my warning perfect for you."

"Perfect for what?"

"Perfect for seeing what you were made of. You might have been up to par for my son's mate, but being a Queen requires sterner stuff. I'm glad to see you have the spirit, at least." Althea gave her an approving look, one that Ximena begrudgingly found she liked.

"Thank you," she said, quietly. "But what does all of this mean for us?" She looked to Blue then and saw that he was now paying attention, his lavender eyes locked on his mother.

"It means we train you. Teach you to lead, and one day when I'm tired and more bored than I am now, I skip off into the sunset and you two are left holding the bag to the fairy kingdom."

"I don't know if that sounds like a good idea, but I'm interested," Blue said, and then looked at her. "Are you?"

"But how are wolves supposed to lead fairies? No one has heard of that being done."

"Doesn't matter if it's never happened before because I, little cub, can *will* anything into existence, and I wish to will this." Althea gave her another glittering smile, reminding Ximena exactly who she was dealing with. The tense moment lasted for only a beat before she leaned back in her throne and gestured excitedly to a side door made of high polished gold. Because in this magical fairy world nothing said personal sitting room like a freaking gold door. "But I would not do such a thing without proper connections and preparations such as this first one!" She waved to the door and called out, "Come in, dear! We are ready for you now."

Ximena and Blue looked in tandem to see the gold door swing open before a pretty dark haired woman walked in and made her way towards them. She looked familiar to Ximena, but that couldn't be. She knew precisely two people, or rather, she did when Blue had been human.

Now that he was a fairy that only left...

"Ximena, hey!" The woman waved excitedly and bounced towards them with an unmistakable energy that had Ximena's mouth dropping open.

"Toni?"

"The one and only, baby!" Toni grinned at her excitedly as she joined them.

"What are you doing here?"

Toni wiggled her eyebrows at her and gave her an impressed look. "I could ask you the same thing. I mean," she held out a hand sweeping it across the richly appointed sitting rooms and then jerked a chin towards Althea, "the fairy queen? Impressive."

"It's...complicated," Ximena sighed, glancing towards Althea. The fairy queen was reclining in her seat and considering them with interest. If she had been bored before her son had claimed his mate, she was at the very least, semi-entertained now. Ximena narrowed her eyes at her. Entertainment...was that why Toni was here?

"Why is Toni here?" Ximena asked, stepping past her self-appointed best friend and towards the Queen.

"I know what you're thinking, but I would never involve your one friend for the sake of entertainment." Althea leaned forward in her chair and rested her chin against her hand with a smile. "I know we have had a bumpy start but we are family now, on account of your love of my son. I would never make you into a game."

"Wouldn't you though?"

"Well," Althea grinned and looked off to the side for a second before her black eyes came back to Ximena, "I would never make a game of the future Queen."

"Wait, you're going to be a Queen?" Toni asked from behind her with a gasp.

"The Fey Queen," Althea called out to her with a look of pride on her face that caught Ximena by surprise.

"Well, shit. That's more than impressive, Xi! That's incredible." Toni clapped her hands in excitement and rushed up towards her. "I'm here to show you how to walk, aren't I?"

Ximena gave her a side long look. "Walk?" she asked. Being a shifter she knew her understanding of the Fey, and much of the supernatural world was lacking. The Bloodstones hadn't cared a bit about the world outside of their existence and it continued to hold her back. Hopefully with her new place in the Fey world that would all come to an end.

She looked towards Althea where Blue was now standing beside his mother. The pair shared a look which had Ximena on alert. Fairies didn't look for fun. There was a message here, something was being communicated, but what? Blue inclined his head towards his mother and Ximena knew she was right. Something was definitely being said. Her focus shifted when Toni touched her arm.

"This is going to be amazing," she gushed.

Ximena frowned in confusion. She had forgotten what Toni was talking about. It was hard to stay on track when there were fairy communications to decipher and all.

"What?"

"Antonia is a Walker. That is why she is here, and walking will be what she teaches you to master."

Ximena's attention flew back to Althea. "Sorry? Walking?"

"Yes, walking. You'll learn to flit back and forth between the dimensions and worlds like a fairy. It will give you the mobility necessary to know when things are going wrong, or to plan. Plus, it's a way to keep the riff raff on their toes," Althea told her while Blue rolled his eyes and came forward to catch Ximena's hands in his.

"Walking is a gift. You will make great use of it. The Oak Fast Walkers are some of the best to learn it from. Toni will teach you what you need to know as quickly as any."

Toni beamed at him. "I am pretty good at my job,

but it never hurts to hear." She paused and gave Blue an assessing look. "You're her mate huh? What's with the human get up?" she asked wiggling her fingers at the human appearance Blue was still in. It was only when Toni asked that Ximena realized he was still wearing it.

Why hadn't he shifted back to his fairy self?

"Oh, right," he looked down at himself and then shrugged, "I forgot about that. I think I'll be keeping it," he said, and then gave Ximena a wink. "It's nice to match my mate."

"I like you both ways," she reminded him, but it was nice to know that he was thinking of her.

"To be honest, I've grown fond of this. However, I will never walk everywhere again. I don't know how you people do it," he told her with a pained look.

She rolled her eyes at his dramatics. "You poor baby."

"I had to walk to town and back. That was," he held up a hand, counting, and then groaned, "that was nearly twenty minutes one way. I thought I was going to lay down and take a nap right there on the sidewalk at one point."

She laughed and hugged him to her. "You fairies need a lesson in keeping focused even when a task is boring."

"That's where you come in. We are a fickle bunch that could do with some toughening up." He kissed her cheek, an arm wrapping around her waist as he turned to look back at his mother. "I blame our current monarch for it."

"Everyone blames the mother," Althea sniffed indignantly. "But I am proud to have you in my family, and as my successor, Ximena. You will make a fine Queen."

"Thank you, Al," she answered. Her chest glowed with pride, and Ximena smiled back at the Queen. This time it was genuine. She did want to make her proud of her, make her glad her son had chosen her, magic or no magic. Blue was her other half, and making his mother happy was an added bonus. But even if the Fey Queen hated her, it wouldn't have mattered. She looked back to Blue and leaned up on her tiptoes to kiss his cheek.

He smiled at her and the love in it hit her square in the chest. No, it wouldn't have mattered if Althea objected with every fiber in her fairy body. Blue was her other half, and Ximena would do anything to protect and honor that. There was no breaking or taking back what they had.

This was forever. And when you dealt with fairies, forever meant precisely that.

Even if she was scared shitless about it, being Queen seemed as good a place as any to start, and so she jerked her chin at Toni and said, "Alright. Teach me how to walk."

Queen Ximena did have a nice ring to it after all.

"You're killing it."

"I walked right into a wall. That's the literal definition of not killing it."

Toni shrugged and popped a gummy bear into her mouth. "I really think this is a matter of opinion, because no one I know has ever been able to phase walk, let alone do it after two days." She tossed a gummy bear at Ximena and said, "Trust me, you're killing it. Even if you did walk into a wall that one time."

The pair were sitting together on a bench in front of Walker Books, they had just finished another training session, the latest in their three week journey into Ximena's education as a future Queen. It was all going well. Ximena was catching onto things a lot faster than she had imagined, Althea was impressed by it, and Blue was smug.

"My mate is brilliant and talented. I expected nothing less."

He was so proud. Ximena loved it when he was proud of her, which was pretty much everyday, and that suited her just fine. They were happy together in their little home on the cul-de-sac she had once thought of as not her home, but just a house.

She'd been wrong then.

Even if she hadn't wanted to admit it. It had always been a home.

Blue brought the wards down and it was like watching people wake up when the neighbors realized they were there, but with a little influence from Blue they all accepted the house and the couple living in it had always been there. Ximena had helped, but her touch at influence wasn't as good as Blue's. With time she hoped it would catch up. He did have a millennia on her after all.

The front door had to be replaced, and while Ximena had liked the yellow door, this time she had opted for a subtly gold hued door. If she were going to be Queen, she might as well learn to be a little extra now, shouldn't she?

She'd caught the neighbors staring at the door more than once.

She spent her time learning what the hell it meant to be a Queen, which was a lot less exciting than someone might imagine. But Blue had been willing to become human to spend a normal lifetime with her, she could do her best to be the best Fairy Queen she could. She was going to be one for a very, very long time. But there was a lot of policy and politics to learn which meant time spent with Althea. They'd become close in those hours spent studying rules and decorum, and Ximena now considered the Fey Queen to be the mother she hadn't had for a long time.

The unpredictable, magic wielding, sharp toothed and black eyed mother she'd never had, actually.

It was a good time really.

Ximena loved their new relationship. Her friendship with Toni was another new relationship she had come to cherish as well. The woman hadn't been kidding when she'd appointed herself as Ximena's best friend, because she had become exactly that in the few short weeks they had begun working together.

Although walking was proving to be challenging and they had only just worked their way to phase walking, which was pretty much teleporting to be honest and so pretty important to keeping that allure of fairy mystery alive. It was kind of neat, really, when Ximena wasn't walking right into buildings, that is. She expected she would have better luck when she managed her connection to Fey magic a little better. It was overwhelming, but she could do it with more practice, or at least Althea assured her she could.

"I've seen it, Xi. You will master this."

She would just have to take the Fey Queen's sight at her word. It's not like she had anyone to ask if it were true. She was the first to do this, which meant a lot of making it up as she went. Good thing she was always up for improvising, and with her mate in her life there was really little she could complain about...even if she was having a little trouble with the phase walking side of things.

Ximena grinned and ate the gummy bear sitting on her lap. "Thanks, it's just hard to keep perspective when I keep---"

"Walking into walls?" Toni offered.

"I thought you just said it was once," Ximena reminded her.

"Eh, maybe it was more than once."

"Whatever."

Toni laughed and shook her gummy bear bag at her. "Listen, let's not nitpick how many times you phase walked into a building, instead lets…" her voice trailed off and she sat up suddenly, "oh, shit."

"What?" Ximena asked following Toni's gaze. "What is it—oh shit!"

"Yeah."

"That's not good."

"Nope.

They were looking at quite the scene. A woman was swinging her purse at a man who was looking like a scolded puppy. He had his head down and his hands up as he tried to come closer, but another swing of the purse showed the woman was having none of it.

"That's a bear," Toni told her, popping another gummy bear into her mouth.

"A bear in trouble," Ximena corrected.

"Oh, what did he do? I'm so nosey, I want to find

out," Toni sighed and looked ready to phase walk right over there, but a loud shout from the woman carried all the information either of them needed to know the hot goss.

"I am not your mate!" The woman practically pinwheeled with her purse swinging out from her arms in an impressive circle. "I don't care what you smell, or what you say, I am not going with you!"

"Looks like...a mate situation." Toni gave her a side-long look. "Should we do something?"

Ximena snagged the gummy bear bag from her and nodded, standing from the bench with a stretch. "Yeah, come on. Can't hurt to make sure she's all right, although at this point I'm thinking we're going over there more to protect that bear."

The woman was swinging her purse so hard that cards, lipstick, and keys were flying out and onto the sidewalk around them while the bear in front of her was still trying to calm her with his hands out as his sides. He looked pitiful. Poor bear.

"He does look stressed," Toni agreed, joining Ximena as they stepped off the curb and onto the street, walking towards the couple. "But how are we going to stop her from knocking him out with that purse of hers long enough to listen?"

"Mates are like that, but I'm sure all they need is a little space and time. I've got an idea about bringing the energy over there down a notch," Ximena said and then she raised her hands over her head and called out. "Hi!

I'm Ximena, the Fey-Queen-in-training. How can I help you today?"

The woman's purse hit the ground with a thud and the bear nearly fell over in shock.

Yeah, she had thought that would stop them long enough to talk.

ABOUT THE AUTHOR

Rebel Carter loves love. So much in fact that she decided to write the love stories she desperately wanted to read. A book by Rebel means diverse characters, sexy banter, a real big helping of steamy scenes, and, of course, a whole lotta heart. Rebel lives in Colorado, makes a mean espresso, and is hell-bent on filling your bookcase with as many romance stories as humanly possible!

Manufactured by Amazon.ca
Bolton, ON

25326988R00083